Also by
MICHAEL LAWRENCE

The Poltergoose

The Killer Underpants

THE TOILET OF DOOM

A JiGGY McCUE STORY

THE TOILET OF DOOM

by **MICHAEL LAWRENCE**

DUTTON

CHILDREN'S

BOOKS

New York

CIP Data is available.

Published in the United States 2002 by Dutton Children's Books,
a division of Penguin Putnam Books for Young Readers
345 Hudson Street, New York, New York 10014
www.penguinputnam.com

Originally published in Great Britain 2001 by Orchard Books, London
Typography by Richard Amari
Printed in USA
First American Edition
ISBN 0-525-46983-4
2 4 6 8 10 9 7 5 3 1

R00200 44985

For Zelda,

who shared the original Stallone

and typed thousands of doomed pages

in a small Welsh coastal town

without complaint

THE TOILET OF DOOM

1

Ever had the feeling your life's been flushed down the toilet? I have. And it wasn't just a feeling. I knew something was wrong the moment I woke up that Sunday morning, but if I'd had the faintest idea *how* wrong I would have jumped straight out of the window onto my mother's favorite rosebush and ended it there and then.

Before I get to the Big Flush, though, I'd better fill you in on how it all started. It was the previous Friday—another day I woke up feeling something wasn't quite right. This time it was my nose. I rolled out of bed and plodded to the bathroom with dread in my heart. The mirror over the basin told me everything I didn't need to know. There was a lump on my nose the size of a satellite dish. "Oh terrific," I said, imagining the day's pathetic jokes at my expense. I left the bathroom.

Left it . . . tripped over something . . . landed nose-first in a big potted plant on the landing.

The day was not starting well.

I pulled my face out of the leaves to see what had tripped me. Our cat, Stallone, lay across the doorway like a draft stopper. He must have seen me go into the bathroom and thrown himself across the door to catch me on the way out. Never misses a chance to trip me up, that cat. Me or Dad. Never trips Mom. He's nice as pie to her. Any female actually. My mother says he's a woman's cat. Dad says they're welcome to him.

"You did that on purpose, you . . . you . . . *animal.*"

Stallone stared back at me with those mean green eyes of his as if to say, "Wanna make something of it, pal?"

The worst of it was the potted plant. It had only been there since yesterday, and suddenly, day two, half its leaves and dirt were on the carpet. Mom would go berserk. I got up and raced to my room. I rummaged under the bed, found what I was looking for: my math book. While I was down there I grabbed the ball of chewing gum I'd been building up piece by piece for months. I licked the dust off and jammed it in my mouth to soften it. It tasted like the inside of a fisherman's boot, but I wasn't rearing it for a taste contest.

4

Another couple of months and my gumball would have been big enough to break some sort of record. Would have. If Stallone hadn't made me use it to stick leaves back on a potted plant.

I was on my knees scooping dirt back in the pot with my math book—at last I had a good use for it—when Dad strolled along the landing in his boxers and "I'm not old, I'm a recycled teenager" T-shirt.

"What happened?"

I took the huge gumball out of my mouth. It wasn't easy. Almost broke my jaw.

"Tripped over cat, fell in plant."

"Your mom'll crucify you."

"Only if we have a snitch in the family," I said, starting on the leaves.

"She won't hear it from me, Scouts' honor."

"Since when were you in the Scouts?"

"What's that got to do with anything? Leaves fell off, did they?"

"Yeah. Sticking 'em back."

"Chewing gum?" I nodded. "Good move," Dad said. "Just what I'd have done."

"When you were a kid, you mean?"

"I mean now. You know what the old girl's like with her rotten plants." He noticed Stallone sprawling across the bathroom door and raised his foot. "Shove off, you!"

Stallone got up, glaring at him with real hatred, and slunk off lashing his tail like a whip.

"Jiggy, are you up yet?"

My mother's voice from downstairs. Dad shot into the bathroom and bolted the door. I looked down. Mom stood at the bottom of the stairs, glaring up at me like I'd committed some crime. I had—the potted plant—but she didn't know that. Yet.

"On my way," I said. She started up the stairs. Panic. There were still some leaves on the floor, and quite a bit of dirt. "I said I'm on my *way!*"

"And I'm coming up to get dressed, d'you mind?" she said.

I grabbed the leaves, crammed them in my mouth— useful things, mouths—chewed like a starving cow, swallowed hard. Then I scooped up the earth and dropped it in my pajama pants. It would have helped if I'd been wearing bicycle clips, but you don't usually get those with pajamas. I headed downstairs, casually rubbing my nose.

"You'll be late," Mom snapped, coming up.

"And good morning to you too," I said, going down.

We drew near. It was going to be a close thing. Half the Garden Center was trickling down my legs. My knees couldn't keep it off the ground forever. But of course Mom stopped. Squinted at me.

"What's that on your nose? Looks like earth."

"Earth?" I said. "Well, thanks very much. I mean I know it's big, but I didn't think it was the size of a *planet*."

I continued down, with no idea that the thing on my nose was going to be the one bright spot of my day. Next six days actually. By this time next week I would have been to hell and back.

Twice.

2

After breakfast I got dressed in time to be almost late for school as usual, said good-bye to my mother, wiped the lipstick mouth off my forehead, and strolled down the path.

"Be careful on the street," she said from the step.

"Mother," I said, walking backward, "this is the Brook Farm Estate. The only things on wheels around here are either parked or retired."

"Still, watch it. Someone gets run over every three minutes in this country."

"He must get pretty sick of it." I crossed the road to Pete and Angie's.

Pete and Angie are my oldest buds. We've known one another since before we were born. They're not related to each other or anything, but they live in the same house, along with his dad and her mom. We call ourselves the Three Musketeers (the kids, not the parents) and we have this Musketeery slogan—"One for all and all for lunch!"—that we cry whenever we leap into action, which is a bit too often for my liking.

They came out seconds before I got to the door. We have this almost-late business down to a fine art. And of course, true to form, the first thing Pete said was: "I like the nose, did you pick it yourself?"

I ignored him. Best thing to do with Pete most of the time. But Angie was looking too. You don't ignore Angie Mint. Not if you want to live.

"Okay," I said. "Get it out of your system."

"Get what out of my system?"

"The stupid remark about my beak."

She looked offended. "I'm offended," she said.

"You are?" I said. "Oh. Sorry."

"I should think so too. I would never be so unkind as to make fun of a face that's been taken over by a giant plum tomato that probably glows in the dark."

"Thanks, Ange."

We set off for school.

"Hey, wait for me!"

We groaned. Eejit Atkins. Ralph to his mom, the teachers, and the social workers. Eejit to his dad and everyone else.

"We'll never get this right," Angie muttered.

What she meant was that ever since Eejit moved in

next door to me we've been trying to get to school without him on our heels and we usually don't make it. It's like he waits for us behind the Atkins family trash can and shoots out the moment we appear.

"Hey, Squirt," said Pete.

Eejit gave him a kick in the shins and swerved so Pete couldn't get him back, then fell into step beside me. Since he became my neighbor he's been treating me like some long-lost relative. I don't encourage him. He chattered like a chipmunk halfway to school while Pete, Angie, and I talked among ourselves, but then he caught sight of a couple of his Neanderthal pals loping along the opposite sidewalk and zigzagged across the road to join them. Traffic swerved.

Reaching school, we jostled our way merrily through the gates. The school gates are about as wide as four kids standing shoulder to shoulder and at the start and end of every day at least sixteen people always want to get in or out at the same time. We broke through without too many personal injuries just in time for the bell, and headed for homeroom.

Friday is a breeze, pretty much, but there's one very tall thin blot on the landscape that spoils the day. Its name is Face-Ache Dakin. Face-Ache is our homeroom teacher, which means that we see more of him than just about any other life-form on Earth. Still, we can handle that. What's harder to handle is that he's also our math teacher, and math is the very last class Friday afternoon. If you know of a neater way to stop the week ending on a high note, keep it to yourself.

The day passed. We snoozed, we shouted, we did a little work. Finally it was time for the Last Lesson. We filed into Dakin's class wishing we were filing the other way. We looked around. Where was he? He's usually there ahead of us, wiping down the blackboard or sitting at his desk writing detention notes in advance, but not today, no sign of him today, so just for once we didn't go all tense and quiet as we crossed the threshold. Some kids—girls mostly—went to their seats and sat like little angels with halos over their heads, but the rest of us just hung out. Pete and I leaned on the window ledge. The view wasn't great, but it was a thousand times better than the one behind us. Just below the window there was this little area called Trash Can Corner. The huge, black trash cans were where all the unwanted food from the school kitchen went. They were pretty full most of the time. Like now. Mr. Heathcliff, the janitor, was down there smashing flies against the cans with a shovel.

"Hey, Mr. Heathcliff!"

He looked up at the sound of my voice. When he saw me leaning out, he hoicked one of the lids off, like he was inviting me to jump. Really terrific joke. He left the lid off, as if to say that I was welcome to take up his offer anytime.

"Seats, everyone!"

Dakin had come in. He was carrying a battered old suitcase. Unusual. Teachers don't often come into class with suitcases. Pete and I went to our seats. I leaned back to talk to Milo, who sits behind me. Milo is Face-Ache's son, poor kid. He's okay, Milo. Doesn't like his old man much more than the rest of us.

"What's the deal with the suitcase, Mile? Don't tell me he's leaving home."

"I wish," Milo said. "I don't know why he brought it. It used to be in my aunt Trixi's antiques shop but it's been under the bed in our spare room ever since it was turned into a Chinese takeout."

"Why was your spare room turned into a Chinese takeout?"

"You two, stop talking!" Dakin bawled. I faced front. He addressed the class. "I have a real treat for all of you today," he said.

"That'll be a change," Bryan Ryan said.

"Watch it, Ryan." Face-Ache hoisted the suitcase on to his desk and opened it. Took out an old book. "*Collier Encyclopedia.* I have a full set here."

He sounded like he thought we'd be impressed. He was wrong.

"Suckered by an encyclopedia salesman," said Dorfman.

"*Really* suckered," said Stefanopoulos. "The jerk didn't even notice they were a hundred years old."

"Not quite that old, Stefanopoulos," Dakin said. "Nineteen fifty-one. And the jerk did know the age, because the jerk bought them from an antiques shop."

"My aunt's," Milo chipped in quietly.

"What I'm going to do is hand these books around for you to study." A hefty groan went up. "Snyder, Gonzalvo, Downey. Here please."

"Why, what have we done?" Downey asked.

"Nothing yet. That's why I want you here."

Snyder, Gonzalvo, and Downey went to the front, where Face-Ache told them to each grab a pile of books from the case and distribute them, one volume per student. The men in charge of encyclopedia distribution headed around the room, dropping the old books on desks.

"Do not *drop* them!" Dakin shrieked. "They are not *litter*!"

They went on dropping them, but more quietly. While they were doing this, Ryan said: "What about the treat, sir?"

"Treat?" said Dakin.

"You said you had a real treat for us."

"This is it. A set of wonderful mid-twentieth-century encyclopedias. Many people never get to see such books these days."

"Looking at ancient books is a *treat?*" Bry-Ry said. "Ever thought of getting a life, sir?"

"How would you like a detention, Ryan?"

"Has to be better than this."

"Fine, it's all yours. See me after."

When Snyder, Gonzalvo, and Downey had dumped all their encyclopedias there were several people without one. Gonzalvo had an opinion about this:

"Math class, and the teacher can't even match the number of kids with the number of lousy books."

Face-Ache was annoyed, probably because Gonzalvo was right. He told him and Snyder and Downey to go back halfway and take one book from every two kids who had one each, and hand one to every two students who didn't have any. This meant that the kids who hadn't got one before had to share one between two now, and so did some of those who'd had one each. Confused? You're in good company. To cap it all, when half the books were redistributed so that every kid either had his own book or one to share with the person next to him, there were six or seven left over.

"What do we do with these?" Snyder wanted to know.

"Burn 'em," said Eejit Atkins.

"Bring them here," said Dakin.

They took them to him. Dropped them on his desk.

"What have old encyclopedias got to do with math, sir?" Kelly Ironmonger asked, as everyone shoved their jaws in the palms of their hands and got set for a massive overdose of boredom.

"We're going to look up mathematicians of the past," said Dakin.

"What for?"

"Everyone should know about the people and events that preceded them." He looked around. "Don't you agree?" No one did. Face-Ache sighed. "You people. You have no curiosity, do you?"

"Sure we do," said Ryan. "We're curious to know why you think we'd be remotely interested in dead mathematicians."

"Going for a double, Ryan?"

Ryan folded his arms and hunkered down in his chair.

"Let's get started," Dakin said. "How many important mathematicians can you think of, class?"

Deafening silence.

"As I thought. Well then, I'll give you some names. We'll start with Steinitz. Ernst Steinitz. Look him up, whoever has the relevant encyclopedia."

Nobody looked him up. Everyone looked at everyone else instead.

"Well, one of you must have it," Dakin said. "None of these covers *S*." He meant the books on his desk. "Who has the volume that covers *S*?" If anyone had it they weren't owning up. "Well, no doubt it'll surface eventually. To get the ball rolling I'll look one up for you. As I have the last volume here, let's see what it has to say about Zariski."

"Never heard of him," said Eejit Atkins.

"Of course you haven't, Atkins," Dakin said, flipping through the *Z*'s. "You're an idiot, why would you have heard of a brilliant mathematician?"

"Hey, that's not fair." This was Angie.

Dakin stopped flipping the *Z*'s. "What's not fair?"

"Calling Atkins an idiot because he hasn't heard of your nerdy mathematician. Atkins is no more of an idiot than the rest of us on this."

Eejit almost burst into tears at such praise. "Hey, thanks, Ange."

"I *mean*," she said, curling a lip at him, "that *no one* has heard of this . . . Zabriski."

"Zariski," Dakin corrected. "'Oscar Zariski,'" he read. "'Russian-American mathematician, 1899 to . . .' Well, he was still alive when this was published. 'Zariski worked out a precise program which showed how every kind of geometric configuration could be discussed in—'"

A phone rang.

Dakin stopped speaking. Stopped breathing. He looked up from the book. His eyes had become dots.

"WHOSE IS THAT?!"

Six boys stood up at once, not to admit that the phone was theirs but to point dramatically at Pete, who was fumbling in his pocket trying to get the thing out. There'd been so many punishments for bringing cell phones into school that hardly anyone did anymore, but Pete loves his phone. He doesn't get many calls but he still loves it.

"Garrett, how many times do you have to be *told*? Bring that thing here!"

Pete got up. Got the phone out of his pocket. It was still ringing.

"And *silence* it!"

Pete punched a button. The ringing stopped. He put the phone to his ear and headed for the front. "What! *What?* Encyclopedias? You're kidding me. Believe me, fella, one thing I don't need right now is encyclopedias." He clicked off.

Dakin snatched the phone and chucked it in a drawer. "Detention, Garrett."

Pete returned to his seat next to me.

"Now I want one of you to read the rest of this article on Zariski," Dakin said. "After that we'll find other articles about other mathematicians and read them."

He looked at the person immediately under his nose: orange-haired, orange-freckled Julia Frame, who sits next to Angie.

"Julia, stand up please, and read what it says here about Oscar Zariski."

He held the encyclopedia out to her. Julia didn't take it. Didn't stand up either.

"Me? Why me? I hate reading out loud. Ask someone else."

"I'm asking you. Come on now. And read clearly so we can all hear."

Julia got up, scowling. She took the book, saw where he pointed, started to mumble.

"I said *clearly*," Dakin said.

"This *is* clearly."

"Not to my ears, it isn't."

"You can get them syringed at the health clinic, sir," I said. "Doesn't hurt, just blows your brains out."

"McCue should know," said Pete. "He's had it done twice."

"Start again," Dakin said to Julia. "And let us *hear* you this time."

Julia started again. We still couldn't hear a word, but no one complained, not even Face-Ache. While she read he chalked names on the blackboard. Names like Gaspard Monge, Julius Plücker, Heinz Hopf, Thomas Bayes, and Pavel Sergeyevich Aleksandrov. (I copied them down so I'd get them right, in case you think I suddenly grew an extra brain.)

"I want you to look these gentlemen up," Dakin said over his shoulder when Julia finally finished telling us about the unfascinating life and works of Oscar Zariski.

No one did a thing except stare without the slightest interest at the weird names on the board. Face-Ache must have sensed this because he stopped writing after about name eight and turned.

"Why is no one looking up any names?"

"You didn't say who had to do the looking," said Snyder.

"Whoever has the right encyclopedia," Dakin said.

Blank stares, slack jaws. Face-Ache put his chalk down.

"Doesn't anyone here know what I'm asking of you?"

A mass classwide shrugging and shaking of heads—and a few grins. We don't often get a chance to have fun with Dakin.

"Me and Jodie Gold know," said Jodie Duthie.

"Praise be," said Dakin. "Which of the names I've written on the board are covered by your encyclopedia?"

"None of them," said the other Jodie.

Dakin closed his eyes for a while. Then he opened them and went through the encyclopedias on his desk. He took one to the Jodies.

"Look up Plücker," he said.

"Clücker?" said a Jodie.

"Plücker. Julius. As on the board."

Jodie and Jodie found the place in the encyclopedia he'd given them, and he tucked their encyclopedia under his arm and went to the window. Jodie Duthie got up and started to read about this old Plücker no one ever heard of before.

While she droned on and Dakin gazed out, some of us saw our chance. Rubber bands sprang into action, and suddenly pellets were whizzing around the room like turbo-driven hornets. Quite a few hit their targets too, but the targets complained silently—until whiny Julia Frame got one in the ear.

"Sir!" she bawled. "Sir, they're being stupid, they're firing things."

Dakin spun around. As he spun, all pellet-firers but one dropped their hands under their desks. The one that didn't was me. I'd been enjoying myself too much to keep more than half an eye on Face-Ache, so he actually saw a pellet fly from my fingers, hit the blackboard, bounce off, and shoot toward him like something from Krypton. He threw his arms across his face, his armpit lost its grip on the encyclopedia, and the encyclopedia flew out the window. As the pellet bounced harmlessly off Dakin's raised arms he jumped around to try and catch the book. Too late. It was already in deep space, spinning over and over, round and round, falling toward . . .

Mr. Heathcliff brought the encyclopedia back up a few minutes later. It was covered in old food from the trash can he'd been reserving for me. It was so disgusting that Dakin wouldn't touch it. He told Heathcliff to put it on his desk.

"Volume thirteen is ruined," he wailed. "Ruined! *Ruined!*"

"Unlucky thirteen," murmured Sprinz.

Naturally, I got detention for firing the pellet that made him drop the encyclopedia in the trash, but at least he gave up trying to teach us about extinct mathematicians. Made us clean the classroom instead. No big deal, you might think, but Dakin's idea of "clean" is Absolute Perfection. We had to measure the distance between the desks with rulers and move them until they were exactly, I mean exactly, the same distance apart. Ditto the chairs. After the desks and chairs we had to go around making sure everything else in the room was just right. He watched us like a stuffed hawk as we rearranged potted plants on window ledges, posters and maps on walls, and made sure all the windows were open the same distance to a sixteenth of an inch. Even the little sticks of chalk in the blackboard tray had to be put in a perfect dust-free line.

3

When the bell rang Ryan, Pete, and I stayed behind. There's a rule at our school that a kid can't do a detention the day he gets it. Has to take a note home to tell his parents he's been Bad and give them a chance to nag him to death for a while. Dakin wrote our notes with a few angry stabs of his pen and threw them at us. "Monday!" Ryan sauntered out like he'd just won the lottery. Face-Ache gave Pete his cell phone back with a warning that next time he'd be stood up against the blackboard and shot.

Angie was waiting for us at the gates. Milo Dakin was with her. Milo had been looking pretty cheesed off all day and looked even cheesier now, which was strange as it was home time.

"Why the face like a horse, Milo?" I said. "You didn't get detention."

"I have detention every day of the week," he said. "You should try living with my dad."

"I'd rather tattoo my chest with a power drill."

Seeing as he was so down we went home his way instead of ours. Bit of a roundabout route but there was no rush. He moaned about his dad every step of the way and we made sympathetic noises to try and cheer him up. Well, Angie and I did. Pete kept rolling his eyes and jerking his head at us to try and get us to turn back and go home a non-Milo way.

"*Fat Chance,* ladies and gentlemen! *Fat Chance!* Help put a roof over someone's head!"

An ultrathin kid of about eighteen with a shaggy black dog shoved a help-the-homeless magazine in our faces. We reared back. Some days you can't move in our town without tripping over *Fat Chance* sellers and their dogs. They always have dogs.

"Got one," I lied to the *Fat Chance* seller and his dog. "At home."

"Oh sure, and where have I heard *that* before?" muttered the *Fat Chance* seller.

"Woof-off," said the dog.

"He's driving me crazy," said Milo as we walked on.

"Yeah, those *Fat Chance* sellers," Pete said.

"He means his dad," Angie said.

"I knew that. Just hoping he'd change the record."

Milo didn't change the record. "I don't know how

much longer I can live my life in alphabetical order," he said.

"Alphabetical order?" I said.

"It's his latest 'Keep Dakin World Tidy' scheme. Everything in my closet and dresser is already color-coordinated, but last night he word-processed all these labels saying 'Handkerchiefs, Pajamas, Shirts, Socks, Underwear.' I mean, does that sound *sane* to you?"

Angie patted him on the shoulder. "Parents and teachers, Milo. Make it up as they go along. Don't let him get you down."

These wise words didn't seem to help. Milo slouched on, dragging his schoolbag. This wasn't like him. He usually managed to put up with his old man. It was hard to know what to say to him when he was in this mood, so we just dragged our bags and slouched with him. It was Angie who broke the slouchy silence.

"Just look at the state of that place. It's like a junk shop."

I glanced at the big new luxury apartment building across the road. It's got a lot of people talking, this place, because no one knows who owns it. Some rich businessman, they say, who stands to make a killing but doesn't want people to know. The apartments aren't for sale, just rent, but a month's rent there would probably buy our entire house and garden gnome.

"The luxury apartment building for filthy-rich people looks like a junk shop?" I said in surprise.

"I mean Mr. Mann's bus shelter," said Angie.

Mr. Mann's bus shelter was on our side of the road, right opposite the luxury apartments. Mr. Mann is the town tramp. He turned up out of nowhere five or six years ago, spent the night in the bus shelter, and never moved out. Summer, winter, heat wave, snow, there he is. Never has a fire, even in really cold weather, just gloves, moth-eaten stocking cap, string around his ankles.

"What I wouldn't give to take a broom and trash can to it," Angie said.

"A match would be quicker," said Pete.

It was a mess, though, no denying it. Piles of old blankets and junk and litter, an ancient bookcase. Mr. Mann's a great one for books. People give him books all the time, and clothes and towels and stuff, though I don't think he ever asks. He has this thick tangled beard down to his waist, and thick tangled hair all down his back, tucked in the belt of his ratty old overcoat, which he wears in all weather. But he's quite popular in spite of the way he looks and the state of his home. When the council tried to evict him last year there was a public outcry, so they dropped the idea and built a new shelter a few yards down for people who actually want to catch buses.

"Hi, Mr. Mann," said Milo.

The raggedy old tramp looked up from his book and smiled.

"Hi, Milo. Good day at the workhouse?"

"Nah. You?"

"Oh, mustn't complain."

Pete and Angie and I kept our eyes on the sidewalk. This wasn't our territory, so we didn't know Mr. Mann to speak to.

"You're very friendly with him," Angie said when the bus shelter was behind us.

"He's a nice man," Milo said. "I pass him twice a day, often stop for a chat." He sighed. "I envy him. No responsibilities, no one telling him what to do the whole time." He sighed again. "Perhaps I should try the Toilet of Life. Never know, might pick up a few tips on how to handle it. Life, I mean."

"What's the Toilet of Life?" Angie asked.

"Computer game. I . . . I know the person who invented it."

Pete whirled around, eyes on springs. "You know someone who invents *computer games?*" It was almost a shout. Pete's a computer game nut.

Milo shrank back in alarm. "He only does it to keep his hand in," he said, like he'd just been accused of something. "He used to be a scientist, something to do with genetics, but then he started his own game company, and—"

He stopped. Seemed kind of embarrassed, like he was betraying some kind of trust by saying all this. Pete wasn't interested in the background info, though.

"This game, this Toilet of Life, what's it do?"

"Never played it," Milo said. "All I know is it's something to do with swapping your life for a better one."

"Which is why you're so tempted," I said.

He grunted.

"But it's only a game, Milo," Angie said. "Won't change anything in the real world."

"No, nothing changes that." He sighed for the millionth time since we left school. "You have no idea what it's like in our house. I can never relax. Everything has to be so *right* all the time."

Pete yawned—loudly.

"I mean *exactly* right," Milo went on. "Like I have to make my bed with the corners tucked under in perfect triangles. And my pajamas have to be folded and smooth like they just came out of cellophane. And doors must be closed without a sound. And lights turned off when you leave the room for ten seconds. And he goes ballistic if I put my elbows on the table at mealtimes. And did you ever hear of anyone else who makes his son eat spaghetti with a knife and fork?"

"Doesn't sound much fun," I said as we turned into Pizzle End Road and approached the Dakin residence.

"It isn't," he said. "Used to drive Mom even crazier than me. I'm not surprised she walked out. Just wish she'd taken me with her, that's all."

"Poor old Milo," Angie said. But it was getting to be a bit of a strain even for her.

We reached his gate, and Pete and Angie and I raised our hands in farewell. They were still in the air when Milo spoke again.

"And proper names," he said.

We lowered the farewell hands. "Proper names?"

"Another rule. Proper names have to be used at all times. Full names. No abbreviations, no nicknames or initials. Like for instance a TV can't be called a TV in our house, oh no."

"So what do you call it," Pete said, "a fridge?"

"A fridge is a 'refrigerator' and the TV is the 'television.' If I ever call it the tube or something he hits the roof."

"He probably just wants you to grow up appreciating

the real names of things," Angie said, not meaning a word.

Milo shook his head. "He was the same with Mom. She had to use the right words too. Everything had to be done the way he said. House had to be spotless the whole time, perfect, in case anyone visited."

"And did they?" I said.

"Did they what?" said Milo.

"Visit," I said.

"Who?" said Milo.

"Visitors," I said.

"No," said Milo. "He wouldn't even let her have a dishwasher."

"The brute," said Angie, and we left him to it before he could get started on the misery of life without a dishwasher.

4

Saturday morning. Fell out of bed and headed for the bathroom to see what the distorting mirror over the basin had to offer. Nothing good. The growth on my schnoz had doubled in size overnight. Soon I'd need a periscope to see over it. But I couldn't burst it. If I burst it I might be scarred for life. Besides, Mom would be in a mood for hours when she saw all the pus on the mirror.

As I left the bathroom I met Dad yawning along the landing. I hadn't told him or Mom about Face-Ache's detention yet because I'd been waiting to get him on his own. When Mom hears I've been in trouble at school she comes over all disappointed and hurt like I'm letting her down personally or something, but Dad can usually handle it. Mom says this is because he's still a big kid himself.

"Hey, Dad," I said. "You know you're always saying

how you used to get detentions at school all the time?"

"Ah yes." His eyes misted over. "Happiest days of my life."

"Well, I got one yesterday. In math. I have a note."

"A note?"

"From Mr. Dakin to tell you I'm in detention after school on Monday. You have to sign it."

"Forge my signature, you know how it goes."

With that, he went into the bathroom and I went back to bed.

An hour later Mom threw my door back. She wasn't happy.

"Jiggy, your father tells me you've been given a detention!"

I covered my head with the pillow. Stupid. Didn't swear him to secrecy. Mom tugged the pillow away and leaned over me with a hefty scowl.

"Well? What do you have to say for yourself?"

"I say it was an accident. I didn't force him to drop volume thirteen."

"I don't know what that's supposed to mean," she said, "and I don't want to. All I know is that you're grounded for the day."

"The day? Today? But Mom, it's Saturday!"

"Yes it is, and you will spend it catching up on all the homework you've so conveniently forgotten."

"But that'll take *years!*"

"Better get started then. And if you don't finish it to my satisfaction today you'll work on it tomorrow too."

I managed to drag out most of the morning by eating breakfast and getting dressed in slow motion, but by early afternoon Mom had cottoned onto my cunning scheme and marched me up to my room and thrown my schoolbooks at me. So there I was, Saturday afternoon, day of rest number one, slaving away in my room and wondering how close I was to dying of boredom. I had my music up really loud to drown out the racket from downstairs. Dad was watching football down there, and when my dad's watching football the last place you want to be is the same house, or even the same street. I looked at the clock on the wall. Five to twelve. Time was really dragging, mainly because the batteries had been dead for weeks. I got up, moved the hands to five past three. "Hmm," I said, "midafternoon. Time to raid the cookie jar."

I headed downstairs.

The noise got more and more unbelievable with every downward step. It was hard to tell who was making the most, the tube or Dad. As I jumped the last three stairs my lunatic father gave a yell so terrifying that I twitched in midair and fell in my second potted plant in as many days. Fortunately, this one was plastic. I picked it up, put it back on its stupid little table, and looked in the living room. There he was, the poor old Golden Oldie, shouting and punching the ceiling like a loon.

"Sad," I said. "Very sad."

I was surprised to see that he wasn't alone today. Stallone was there too. Stallone usually makes himself scarce when football's on, like me when I have a choice—like my mother, who'd gone to the Garden Center where she practically lives. But today Stallone was in and he didn't look too pleased about the peace-and-quiet famine.

Before I go any further I'd better tell you how we came to be the proud owners of a cat like Stallone. Before him, we'd only had one pet. A budgie. We got the budgie because one day Mom said she needed someone sensible to talk to. Dad was happy enough about the budgie plan because budgies don't cost a lot. He got a bit less happy in the pet supermarket, though, when he realized that you can't buy a budgie without also buying a budgie cage, a budgie bell, a budgie mirror, a budgie ladder, and some millet. But it was too late to back out by then because Mom had fallen in love with this cute little blue fella. Dad wanted to call him Schwarzenegger but Mom preferred Beaky. Mom won, as usual. Beaky turned out to be the perfect name, as it happens, but we didn't know that at the time. Beaky the Blue Budgie had only been with us a couple of days when my grandparents turned up without an appointment. They brought us a present, something they thought we'd really like: a half-wild alley cat. One look at those hard green eyes and that bristling fur and Dad said, "Stallone. We're going to call him Stallone." The new addition to the McCue household bared his teeth and spat at him. Dad spat back. It was hate at first sight. But next morning Stallone seemed much more relaxed. Pretty pleased with himself too. Wasn't hard to see why. Beaky's cage was empty. All that was left of our poor little birdie was a few blue feathers waving about in the budgie droppings at the bottom. And his beak, clinging to the bars.

Anyway. Saturday afternoon, Stallone home, Dad bawling at the TV. You could tell Stallone didn't appreciate the commotion by the way he stood on his claws, eyes like killer zap guns aimed at the middle-aged hooligan on the couch. Dad wasn't aware of the effect he was having on the family pet. Too busy jumping up and down and screaming himself hoarse with his arms in the air.

He got a bit more aware when Stallone cracked, though. With an ear-splitting squeal of rage the furious beast flew across the room, landed on the innocent football fan's chest, and drove his claws deep into the armpits on either side. Dad's new scream wasn't much different from the old one except there was a tad less joy in it. The mad feline must have sensed that he'd overstepped the mark because the scream was still bouncing around the wallpaper when he raced back across the room and jumped out the window.

"That's it!" Dad shrieked. "That cat is going to the vet's!"

I went to the window. "No, he's going the other way." But then I realized what he meant. I turned in horror. "Dad, you wouldn't."

He looked from one armpit to the other. Blood was seeping through his shirt. "Watch me," he growled.

"You can't," I said. "I mean yes, okay, he went a little over the top just then, but that's no reason to have him put down. Couldn't you just, say . . . cut his meat ration for a while?"

Dad looked up from his armpits. His eyes were almost as red as they were. He gave a dry little chuckle like a warped genius who's just worked out how to destroy the world and make a profit.

"I won't have him put down. Too good for him. No. I'll have him done."

"Done?"

"Neutered. Snipped. If that doesn't calm him down, nothing will. It'd certainly take the edge off my day."

But then a dim little spot of sanity returned to his eyes.

"Don't tell your mother, though, will you? She wouldn't approve."

"You told her about my detention."

He looked suddenly shifty. "I had to. Can't keep school stuff from your mom, you know that. Has to know how you're doing all the time. And I didn't tell her what you did to her plant, did I?"

"Only because a miracle occurred and she didn't notice. Anyway that wasn't my fault. Stallone tripped me."

"Stallone again," Dad said. "You have to admit, that cat's a liability. If we have him seen to he'll be calmer. Less mean. Come on, Jig, say you won't tell your mom Stallone's heading for the nutcracker."

"She's bound to find out sooner or later," I said. "Probably next time he rolls on his back with his legs all over the place."

The mad look flashed back into his eyes. A thin tight smile jerked his lips to left and right.

"By then it'll be too late. The little monster'll be as docile as a fluffy pillowcase."

With that he fell back on the couch looking from one bloody pit to the other, and began whimpering quietly. Something happened on the TV that turned the crowd hysterical. Dad didn't hear. Didn't notice.

5

Angie helped me with my homework for a couple of hours. On the phone. She's better than me at math, science, history, geography, and woodwork theory. When Mom returned from the Garden Center and found Dad moaning on the couch, she drove him to the hospital for a tetanus jab. Dad usually drives when they go out together but she thought he might have a bit of a problem with his arms sticking out of the sunroof. When she brought him back his arms were down but they still wouldn't hang properly because the bandages in his pits were the size of bricks. Dad came up and looked in on me, still hard at work with Angie on my rotten homework.

"Has the vicious little fiend come back yet?"

"Haven't seen him. Probably keeping out of your way."

"Very wise," he said, and went.

"What was that all about?" Angie said in my ear.

"Tell you later."

I was all set to slip over to hers and Pete's after dinner when my mother threw herself across the front door.

"Oh no you don't, my lad. Grounded I said and grounded I meant."

"Until I caught up on my homework, you said."

Her face went all narrow and suspicious. "Are you saying you have?"

"Absolutely, now move aside please."

"You're not leaving this house until I've checked it over."

"The house?"

"The homework. If it's not good enough you can do it again."

She armlocked me up to my room and went through my homework so slowly the hands on my dead clock moved faster. She made me do a couple of bits again too, so it was getting late by the time I was finally allowed out.

Across the street I rang Pete and Angie's doorbell. Pete and Angie's bell is black-and-white plastic, like all the others on our side of the estate. On the other side— over on Madonna Way and Brad Pitt Close—the bells are solid brass. They also have four bedrooms, double garages, and better trash cans. You don't want to stand in the street for more than two seconds over there in case you get dragged off as litter.

Pete opened the door. He had a can of nondiet something in his fist.

"Hi, scum."

"Whose room?" I said, barging past him.

"Mine, I'm on the computer."

We started up the stairs. "Where's Angie?"

"Bath, hair wash. Usual Saturday-night girlie stuff. That's really coming along."

"What is?"

"The giant fairy light on your nose."

Up in his room he flopped into the swivel chair in front of his PC.

"What are you doing?"

"Writing in my diary," he answered, typing.

"You keep a diary? You've never said. What do you put in it?"

"All the really terrific and exciting stuff that happens around here."

He leaned back so I could read what he'd just written.

Saturday. Did nothing. Evening. Jiggy here. Typed this.

"And these are the best years of our lives," I said sadly.

"Hey—life!" Pete said.

"What about it?"

"That game Milo mentioned. The Toilet of Life. Let's look it up."

I'm not into computer games myself, but there wasn't really anything else to do, so I said: "OK." And with those two simple letters—O and K—I sealed my fate. If I'd had any idea what was going to happen I would have run from that room, that house, and locked myself in our garden shed until Thanksgiving. But I didn't run. I waited while Pete called up Socrates, his favorite search engine. Watched as he typed "Toilet of Life" in the search window and clicked "Find exact phrase." When a door appeared on the screen I was still there.

"What now?" I said. Stupid! Stupid!

There was a sign on the door, which said VACANT. Pete clicked the sign and the door swung inward. We were now looking at a large toilet with the seat down. Scrawled on the wall behind the toilet, like graffiti, were the words:

The Toilet of Life
A Manx Game

There were no instructions, no clues as to what to do next, so Pete clicked around a bit. Nothing happened until he clicked on a little handle over the toilet. The handle moved, the toilet flushed, and suddenly the screen was packed with all these much smaller toilets with their seats down. Not just toilets, though. Walking around them, weaving in and out of them, were all these little people—men in suits, women in skirts, old fogeys with walkers, kids blowing bubble gum—all sorts, like you see in any street.

"Interesting," said Pete.

"Am I missing something?" I said.

He started clicking again, all over the screen. At first the result was the same as before—nothing—but then one of the tiny toilet seats flew up and the nearest little person gave a yelp and jumped headfirst into the bowl. He was halfway in, legs kicking wildly, looked stuck there, but then there was this miniature flushing sound and he slithered all the way down.

"How did you do that?" I asked.

"Dunno, but if I can do it once . . ."

He clicked away, searching for the hidden trigger that made the little people jump into the toilets and get flushed. A second seat flew up. A second little person yelped, jumped in, kicked, and was flushed away.

"Think I've got it," Pete said, and clicked some more.

A third seat flew up, person three yelped, jumped in, got flushed. Pete gave a whoop. He'd gotten it all right. He got busy.

"Hey, Jig."

I turned with relief as Angie came in. Her hair was up in a towel and she was wearing shiny black pajamas covered in stars and planets and comets and stuff.

"Hey, Ange. Cool pj's."

She plucked at the shiny black material. "Cool?"

"Don't you like them?"

"If I had an ambition to be launched into space as a satellite I'd be over the moon about them, but as I don't . . ."

"So why are you wearing them?"

"Because my mother bought them specially. From a catalog, sight unseen." She gave me that long-suffering look we use when our mothers splat into the conversation. "What's he up to?" she said, glancing at Pete's screen.

"That game Milo Dakin was thinking of trying. The Toilet of Life."

"Any good?"

"Nah. Just another zapfest. Death and destruction but with toilets."

We looked for somewhere to sit. This is always a problem in Pete's room because he likes to decorate the carpet with clothes, comics, and all sorts of junk that wouldn't look out of place in Mr. Mann's bus shelter. The only other place to sit was the bed but you wouldn't catch us on that—Pete's disgusting feet had been in it—so we cleared a space on the floor and parked our back ends. While Pete flushed and whooped like a maniac in the corner I told Angie about Mad-Cat Stallone and my father's armpits.

"He says he's going to have him vetted," I said. "Stallone's privates are going to be toast."

"Bit drastic."

"Yeah, but it's his own fault. I mean if you're a cat and you live in someone's house, rent-free, all meals included, own litter box, you can't go around shredding their armpits whenever you feel like it."

"Personally I think he showed quite a lot of self-control," Angie said.

"How do you figure that?"

"Well, if I was a cat stuck in a room with your dad while he's watching football I'd skip the armpits and go straight for the throat. That'd shut him up."

"Come and look at this," Pete said.

"We're not interested in people being flushed down toilets," I said.

"The people are all flushed. Now another toilet's turned up, with a message."

"What kind of message?"

"Come see."

We got up, schlepped across the room, looked at the screen. The people and all the little toilets had disappeared. Their place had been taken by a much bigger toilet, a twin of the one we'd found behind the VACANT door. Wafting around it was a banner with these words:

Feel that your life has gone down the toilet?
Well, here's your chance to swap it
for a better one! Invite someone in who's
really got it made, hit "F for Flush," and . . .

"So this is what Milo meant," I said.

"Yeah," said Pete. "And like he said, it's tempting. Very tempting."

He stretched a finger toward "F for Flush."

"Leave it alone," Angie said. "We don't know what it is."

"Yes we do," he said. "It's a harmless computer game."

"Well, leave it just in case."

But she was curious, and maybe she would have let him hit "F for Flush" if he hadn't been interrupted by a shout from downstairs.

"Pete! Why haven't you done the dishes yet?"

Pete went to the door. "Five minutes, Dad!"

"No minutes! It's your turn to do the dishes and they should have been finished by now. Kitchen, five seconds, or you're in the deep stuff!"

"Talk about timing," Pete said. He started to leave, but came back. "Nobody hit 'F for Flush' while I'm gone—all right?"

"Wouldn't want to," Angie said.

Pete went. I leaned over his empty chair. Peered at the toilet on the screen. The seat was quivering, like it was itching to open. My "F for Flush" finger twitched. I didn't know it but I was seconds away from a fate I wouldn't wish on my worst enemy. Well no, that's not quite true. It would have made my year to see Bryan Ryan get what was going to happen to me.

"Don't, Jig," Angie said. "I have a funny feeling about this."

"It's just a gimmick," I said. "Come on, let's try it."

"It says 'Feel that your life has gone down the toilet?' Your life isn't so bad."

"Not so bad? With a homework tyrant for a mother, an armpit-eating cat, and a meteorite on my nose? Swap with you any day."

"At least you have a *father*," Angie said.

"He's all yours," I said, and hit "F for Flush."

The toilet seat flew up and a bright blue cloud shot out. The cloud fanned across the screen until it filled it, corner to corner, and then . . .

. . . it started spewing into the room.

"Told you something would happen," Angie said.

"But it's a computer game," I said. "No computer game is so interactive it can come into the room."

More and more of the blue stuff seeped out. We backed away.

"Didn't Milo say the friend who invented it used to be some sort of scientist?" Angie said.

"So?"

"So maybe he added something extra. Something to make it *really* interactive."

We stopped backing away. Not because we wanted to but because the wall didn't seem to like the idea of us backing through it. We glanced toward the door. The cloud swirled between us and it.

"Only other way out is the window," I said. (The blue cloud hadn't gotten that far yet.)

"It's quite a drop," Angie said.

"Better than being suffocated by this stuff."

We headed for the window. Too late. The blue cloud got there first. We were trapped.

"When we get out of here," Angie said, "I want you to remind me to do something."

"What?"

"Remove your teeth with pliers one by one, and play pool with your eyeballs."

We were still standing there wondering what to do next when the two halves of the cloud joined up and covered us. It was like being in a blue fog. A fog so dense that we couldn't see one another. Then all these sparkly bits started appearing, and bursting—*pop-pop-pop*—like thousands of tiny balloons. And when they burst . . .

"What a *smell!*" Angie's voice said from somewhere near.

She was right. No nostril could survive that for long. *Pop-pop-pop.*

"I'm out of here," I said, groping for the door through the blue fog.

Instead of the door I found Angie, also groping. We slapped each other's hands for a while, then yanked the door back and stepped outside. As we closed the door to keep the smell and the cloud in, the Toilet of Life flushed—loudly. We stumbled downstairs, ripped the front door open, and gulped air.

"What's with you two?"

Pete stood behind us in rubber gloves ten sizes too big for him, dripping all over the floor. We ignored him, carried on gulping.

"Hello, what's this?" Not Pete this time. Angie's mother, Audrey.

"Terrible smell," Angie said. "In Pete's room."

"Don't look at me, I wasn't even there," Pete said.

Now Oliver, his father, joined us. It was turning into quite a party.

"What was that about a smell? Not gas?"

"Bit like it," I gasped.

Oliver frowned. "Could be gas. New house, cowboy builders . . ."

"Better go and look," Audrey said.

"Me?" he said.

"Well, you're the man."

"Oh, I see. So it's all right for me to get blown to smithereens, being a man, but not you, being a woman."

But up he went, knowing he'd never hear the last of it if he didn't. Pete's dad and my dad have a lot in common.

"Feel sorta queasy," Angie said quietly.

"So do I," I said. "And . . . sleepy."

Oliver reappeared on the landing. He looked relieved. "Not gas. Hardly any smell at all. Just the famous Pete Garrett foot-rot aroma."

Angie yawned. "Anything else there? Like a sparkly blue cloud?"

"Not that I noticed. Just this jazzy sort of pattern on Pete's computer."

"What have you *done*?!" Pete said, and flew upstairs in his oversized rubber gloves.

"Gotta hit the sack," Angie said.

"Me too," I said.

She set off up the stairs, clawing the banister. I stumbled out into the street wishing I had a banister to claw. In two minutes I was home, up in my room. In three I was hopping about trying to slot my feet in my pajama legs. In four and three-quarter minutes I was in bed. In five I was sleeping peacefully. Well, not *so* peacefully. I had a dream. A dream that I was being pulled down into this enormous toilet by grasping hands.

And flushed away.

6

And now we come to the morning it all *really* started. I woke up feeling kind of strange. Not myself somehow. But at least it wasn't a school day. Mom wouldn't be yelling for me to get up, not for a while anyway. She couldn't leave me entirely in peace, though. It really annoys my mother when people are in bed and she's not. My head was deep inside the comforter, along with the rest of me, when I heard her voice somewhere on the other side of it.

"Jiggy, your father's gone to play touch football and I'm off to the Garden Center to look at sprinklers. Don't lie there all day."

I waited for the front door to slam before heading for the bathroom to make a sprinkler of my own. I still felt sort of peculiar, like part of me was . . . well, missing. One thing that was definitely missing was the growth on my nose. Good news, I thought, stroking my smooth lump-free beak.

I was almost at the bathroom when I caught a sly movement on the stairs. Stallone—creeping up toward me. First I'd seen of him since yesterday. He'd probably slept in some alley to keep out of Dad's way. But he was back now, and looking at me. A shiver of fear tap-danced through me. Perhaps the great armpit massacre had given him a taste for human blood. Perhaps he wanted some of mine now. But he didn't attack me. Far from it. When he got to the top of the stairs he wound himself around my ankles; wound so tight I couldn't go another step. And purred. If you knew Stallone you'd know how rare this is. Purring just never happens, not when he's near me or Dad. But I saw what he was after. He wanted to get me on his side.

"It won't work," I told him. "I have no sympathy for you. You have only yourself to blame, Stallone. Only yourself."

I eased my ankles out of his tight furry grip to stop myself going downstairs before I was ready, and continued along the landing for six full inches before I heard what I'd just said and came to a shocked halt. Well, not *what* I'd said, but *how*. What was wrong with my *voice*?

The phone on the wall rang. I considered ignoring it, but it kept on ringing, so I grabbed it to shut it up.

"What!"

"Jiggy?"

"Who's that?" I said with my new peculiar voice.

"Angie."

"You don't sound like Angie."

"You don't sound like Jiggy. We have to meet. Come to the door."

"The door?"

"Tall narrow thing made of wood at the front of your house."

"Soon as I'm dressed," I said.

"Come as you are!" she yelled, busting an eardrum. *"NOW!!!"*

The phone died. I looked at the receiver. I had no interest in the receiver, but in films and on TV people always look at telephone receivers when the person at the other end hangs up. I've never understood this. I mean, what do they think it's going to do—apologize?

I jogged downstairs. I've done this a million times but today it felt all wrong, like my lower decks had gone into a coma.

I looked at the closed front door. Nervously. The front door is not one I often open in my pajamas. This is mainly because pajama bottoms have a way of springing apart just as the whole world walks by with a poodle. I snatched a picture of my grandma off the wall and put her over my fly. I opened the door. Across the road Pete and Angie's door was already open. Someone stood there looking at me. Someone in snazzy black pajamas with stars and planets all over them. Not Angie, though. Someone else entirely.

Me.

I clutched the door handle to stop my knees giving way. As I clutched, I half turned and caught a glimpse of myself in the mirror that hung on the wall next to where my grandma's picture wasn't.

The face in the mirror wasn't mine.

It was Angie's.

I looked back across the road. At myself in Angie's fancy pj's. I was puzzled. Too puzzled for the moment to be horrified. Horror would start about twenty-five seconds later when it sank in. Well, I ask you. Would *your* mind be working on full power if you'd just woken up and discovered that you'd switched bodies with the kid across the road?

A kid of the opposite *sex*?

7

Angie and Pete came over ten minutes later. Angie had ditched the snazzy pj's, but the clothes she'd put on instead looked all wrong, mainly because the clothes were a girl's and the body wasn't. I hadn't gotten dressed. There hadn't been time. I'd spent the first six minutes gulping at the mirror and the other four dealing with an emergency in the bathroom.*

Naturally Pete found it all a real hoot. Mentality of a gnat, that kid. It was all right for him, he still had his own body, but it was no picnic for me having to walk around with Angie Mint's girlie apparatus. You don't need sex-education lessons to know there are serious differences between boys and girls. Actually, knowing all the gory details made it even worse somehow. I'd seen the diagrams. I'd read the labels. I'd looked at the pictures of the internal workings with a magnifying

---

* I won't go into that if you don't mind.

glass. All the boys had. But now that I was so close to everything, using it like it was my own, I felt kind of . . . unwell.

I soon found out that Angie didn't feel much happier, even though she had the better end of the deal.

"This is your fault," she said, with my voice.

"How do you figure that?" I said, with hers.

"Well, it wasn't me who hit 'F for Flush.'"

"You think the Toilet of Life did this?"

"Can you think of anything else that's invited you to swap lives with the person standing next to you recently?"

"Lives," I said. "Didn't say anything about bodies."

"Same difference. I told you not to fiddle with it, but would you listen? Oh no."

"Lynch him," said Pete.

"Thanks, Pete," I said.

"Guillotine him," he said. "Shoot him," he added. "Put him in a bag and throw him in the river. Send him to the electric chair."

"Electric toilet might be more appropriate," I said.

"Please don't say that word," said Angie.

"Electric?" I said. "Appropriate?"

"Toilet."

"You don't want me to say 'toilet'?"

"No."

"Why, what's wrong with 'toilet' all of a sudden?"

"Just don't say it, all right?"

"Okay, I won't say 'toilet' again."

"Make sure you don't."

"Not a single 'toilet' shall pass these lips. Not one 'toilet.'"

"It *keeps* passing your lips. My lips."

"'Toilet'? Does it?"

"Will you shut up? I'm almost wetting myself here."

"So why don't you go to the 'toilet'?"

She aimed a swipe at my head. I ducked just in time.

"I wonder," said Pete.

We looked at him, shocked. It's not often Pete wonders.

"Wonder what?" I said.

"If the Toilet of Life could be some new kind of computer virus."

"Computer viruses ruin your hard disk, not your life. Corrupt your files, not your genes."

"Yeah, but technology's advancing all the time. Never know what they'll come up with next. If it's a virus that can travel around the Internet and infect people through their home computers . . . wow, talk about progress!"

"Progress?" Angie and I said, gazing helplessly at our

bodies on the wrong people. "Well, progress or not," she said then, "until we figure out what to do about it we have to pretend to be each other."

"Why do I have to pretend to be one of you?" Pete asked.

"Not you, nitwit. Come on," she said to me, "we have to swap clothes."

"You want to swap *clothes* with me now?" I said in dismay.

"We have to. Go. Shoo. Upstairs."

We went up. Pete too, chuckling quietly.

"I think we need a few ground rules in case we can't reverse this for a while," Angie said as we reached the landing.

"What sort of ground rules?"

"No peeking, for one. That's my private property you have there, copyright Angie Mint. If you have to get changed in daylight or with the light on, keep your eyes on the ceiling. No taking baths or showers either. At last you have a genuine excuse. You only do stuff you really have to, and you don't take your time doing that. Got it?"

"Got it," I said, "and ditto." We went into my room. "In fact double ditto. You have a free extra attachment I wish I didn't have to mention."

I handed her the clothes I'd thrown at the chair the night before.

Angie curled my lip. "I'm not wearing those; they've been used."

"I was never that picky when I was a boy," I said, but hauled out a clean shirt, jeans, socks, underpants.

She reared back from the last of these. "You can keep the undies," she said.

"It's all right. They're new. My mother bought forty-four assorted pairs of fire-damaged pants from this vandalized-warehouse sale. I've got enough underpants to last three twelve-year-olds into old age. Besides, you have to wear some. They're specially designed to cope with the free extra attachment."

"The escape route comes in handy," Pete informed her.

Angie snatched the clothes, including the fire-damaged underpants, and flung herself out of the room. I flung myself after her.

"Where are you going?"

"Bathroom. To change."

"I've seen it all before, you know. Quite often actually."

"Not on me, you haven't." She was about to go in when she thought of something. "Jig, you haven't . . . you know, been to the . . . ?"

"Had to," I said. "Don't worry, I sat through the whole thing."

She slammed the door. Half a minute later it opened a fraction, and I was leaping in all directions trying to catch the clothes she slung out.

"Clean on fifteen minutes ago," she said, and slammed the door again.

Clean or not, I kicked her underwear into the Twilight Zone under my bed. Pete watched me, grinning.

I pointed at the door. "Out!"

He went. I got dressed. As quickly as I could with my eyes shut. I'd had about twenty minutes to get used to this by now but I still couldn't believe it was happening. I mean, imagine. There you are, a boy all your life, you hit the hay one night, and next morning there's a lot of slack in the fire-damaged underpants. Something like that takes some adjustment.

When Angie came out of the bathroom in my clothes she marched straight up to me and swiped me around the head again. This time she got me.

"What was *that* for?" It might have been her head but it was me who felt it.

She pointed angrily at her new nose.

"Oh, that," I said.

"Yes, that."

The thrill of finding I'd turned into a girl in my sleep had put the nose bump quite a way down my list of things to get excited about. It was so big today, so red and squishy, that you couldn't call it just a spot anymore. No.

"It's a boil," I said.

"Very big boil," said Pete.

"Big as a house," I said.

"A mansion," said Pete.

"And guess what, Ange," I said.

"What?" she said.

"It's all yours."

8

We considered telling our parents what had happened. But not for long. You can't tell your Golden Oldies you've swapped bodies with a neighbor and expect them to carry on as usual. Their poor old brains can't handle stuff like that. No, this was something we had to deal with ourselves.

"We need to think this through," I said. "But not here. I don't know what I'd do if Mom or Dad waltzed in and saw me like this."

"They'd think you were me," Angie said.

"Exactly. We need to be on neutral ground while we get used to all this."

"Lots of neutral ground in the park," she said.

"Fine."

"Have to be careful on the way, though. Pretend we're who we look like in case we bump into anyone we know."

"No problem for me," said Pete.

"You mean if we meet someone I have to talk to them the way you would?" I said to Angie.

"Not just talk, you have to *be* me. If you look like me but act like you people will think something's up."

"Something *is* up, Ange. Very up."

"Yes, well let's stop whining and make the best of it, shall we?"

"Best?" I said. "What best? There is no best."

She came over all fierce. "Pull yourself together, McCue. Where's your backbone?"

"Turn around, I'll show you."

But I saw her point. If we didn't act like each other people might stare. Then they might start asking questions. Whatever happened we didn't want questions. Questions could make us a laughingstock. Two laughingstocks. We left the house and set off, trying to be each other. It wasn't easy. I mean I've known Angie since before I can remember, but I've never taken much notice of the way she moves and all. She seemed to be having a bit of trouble being me too.

"Angie," I said, "don't take this the wrong way, but put a lid on the strut, eh? You're killing my image here."

She narrowed my eyes at me. "What do you mean?"

"Well, Jiggy McCue's a pretty cool dude, and—"

"News to me," said Pete.

"—and cool-as-a-cube Jig just doesn't walk like that."

"So how am I walking that's so uncool?"

"Kind of hunched over and swinging my arms like something in a wildlife documentary with fleas. This isn't a criticism of you personally, you understand."

"What about you, then? You've started to mince."

"Mince?"

"Walk with dear little steps and waggle my hips."

"Get outta here."

"He is, isn't he?" she said to Pete.

"Haven't noticed. Walk up and down," he said to me.

"No."

"Come on, man. Cause of science and all."

So I walked up and down a couple of times.

Pete nodded. "Mincing like a maniac."

"Look, I'm doing my best here," I said. "You think it's *easy* being a female?"

"Half the population seem to manage it," Angie said.

"The other half. And will you stop doing *that*?"

"What now?"

"Pouting."

"I do not pout!" she said, pouting like a porpoise.

"Didn't used to, not so I noticed anyway. Maybe my lips don't agree with you."

"Don't get your undies in a knot, Jig," Pete said with a punchable smirk.

By this time we were doing our bad impressions of each other very close to the fateful spot where Milo had told us about the Toilet of Life. On the other side of the road was the luxury apartment building and on our side was Mr. Mann's bus shelter.

"Wonder who he is?" Angie said.

"Mr. Mann," I said.

"I mean the guy talking to him."

The guy talking to Mr. Mann was an official-looking type in a suit who'd just taken a batch of papers out of his briefcase for Mr. Mann to look through.

"Probably from the council," Pete said. "Sent to have another stab at getting him to move."

"On a Sunday?"

"Overtime."

The council type took a pen out of his pocket and handed it to Mr. Mann, who scribbled something on one of the papers.

"Probably just signed his own eviction notice," Pete said.

"Poor old boss," said Ange.

"Or death warrant," said Pete.

"Hi, Angie. I've never seen you over this way before."

We turned. It was Julia Frame of the orange hair and freckles who sits next to Angie in class. Julia really irritates Angie. Whenever she's in a bad mood Julia tries to cheer her up with hugs and little songs, and Angie wants to thump her. Suddenly I understood this. Here we are trying not to meet anyone we know and she pops up out of the blue with a bunch of flowers, smiling. At me.

"Shove off, Jools," I said. "We're having a private conversation here."

Julia's sugar-sweet smile puckered. The flowers fell to her side.

"I only said hello."

"Yeah, well who asked you to?"

Her forehead turned to corrugated paper. Her bottom lip trembled. "Why are you always so mean to me?" she said.

I glanced at the others. Pete was grinning his head off, but Angie's expression wasn't so easy to read, even though it was one of mine. Was that admiration I saw in my eyes? She spoke to Julia like that all the time. Maybe she was impressed. Thought I was doing a good job of being her.

"Mean?" I said to Julia. "You ain't heard nothing yet. You want mean, stick around. If you don't, let's see your dust."

A tear jumped into one of her eyes. She blinked. A tear jumped into her other eye. She blinked again. Then both tears jumped out and jogged down her cheeks.

"But I lent you my Barbie pencil sharpener."

"And . . . ?" I said.

"Well, I don't lend just *anyone* my pencil sharpener."

"I'm touched. Now beat it or I call the cops."

A little sob burst like a bubble from her mouth. She spun around and walked away with her head about waist-high. I felt good about that for three whole seconds. Then I started feeling a bit less good. Then I became guilty as hell. Pete's grin was even broader now. For some reason I couldn't look at Angie. I felt—don't laugh—ashamed.

"Hey, Julia!" I yelled after her. "Nice flowers! Who are they for?"

"They're for someone who *cares* about me!" she shouted back with a trembly voice. "My grandma, for her birthday! She's over fifty, she'll be dead soon, then I'll be really upset and you can make even more fun of me!"

It was all I could do not to break down myself as she walked away. Me, Jiggy McCue, all set to blub his eyes out. Well, Angie's eyes. Hey now, wait. What was going on here? Angie never got all emotional about stuff, not sloppy emotional, but I was using her equipment, so why had Julia gotten to me when she wouldn't have gotten to Ange? I needed to think about this. But not now. I hauled a smirk on to my borrowed chops to cover my tracks.

"That girl's a nutcase," I said, super-cool.

I glanced at Pete, expecting him to agree with me. His grin was gone. He was gaping at me in horror.

"Nice *flowers*? Since when did you notice *flowers*?"

"Well, I . . ."

He was right, of course. I'm a boy. Flowers live in another universe. I looked at Angie. Her expression was easy enough to read now. It told me that she knew what I was going through. Knew but wasn't sympathetic. Suddenly I realized something. Angie had all the emotional stuff that girls are born with but she didn't give in to it. She kept it inside, down deep, refused to let it out. Looking at her now, head held high, shoulders back, you'd never have guessed she was a girl this time yesterday. She made a much better boy than I ever did.

9

It wasn't until we were almost at the park that I realized I wasn't living up to my name. I mean I'm not called Jiggy for nothing. For the first two or three years of my life I couldn't keep still for a minute. My parents thought there was something wrong with me. They took me to experts. The experts were stumped. Whatever they were expert in, it wasn't perfectly healthy young kids who have to keep on the move without a break, day and night. Then they came to this Big Conclusion. "He has too much energy, but he's too lazy to put it to proper use." What they meant was that instead of doing normal boy stuff like getting into fights and kicking balls around between meals I danced on the spot and made rapper-type arm movements all over the place. I've got it pretty well under control these days, but I still move around quite a bit when stuff happens. Turning into a girl without an operation should have sent me jigging all the way up to the roof, you'd think.

But it didn't. That's what I realized as we approached the park. I wasn't jigging at all. Hadn't so much as twitched since Angie and I traded bods.

"Angie," I said as we went through the park gates, "how do you . . . you know . . . feel?"

"Feel?" she said. "Oh, wonderful. Great. It's always been my wildest dream to look like you."

"No, I mean you don't feel kind of . . . jiggy?"

"Didn't I just answer that? I feel *very* Jiggy."

I gave up.

The Councillor Snit Memorial Park is quite big and open, with trees and grass and bright things with petals and all. Parts of it, the really ancient parts, have been there since the Golden Oldies were kids. The newer parts have tennis courts and a kiddies' play area and a little café that's never open because they can't get slave labor. We went to the little café that's never open and sat on some hard iron chairs under a tree. The chairs are bolted to the ground so no one can steal them. Not only can you not steal them but you can't turn them around to face your friends, so you have to sit all in a row looking at other things, like bushes. Actually I was quite glad of this because sitting in a straight line helped me not look at Angie. Let me tell you, it's no fun sitting next to yourself and having to look yourself in the eye. Couldn't help the odd glance, though. Oh, but she was a handsome devil, even with that thing on my nose. I mentioned this so she wouldn't get self-conscious about it.

"Heck of a boil, Ange."

"Like I need reminding," she said.

"You won't burst it, will you? Promise you won't burst it. I mean I know it's huge and horrible and makes you look really, really gross, but it could look a million times worse if you burst it."

"I have no intention of bursting it," she said, all hoity-toity. "I do not burst boils. I don't usually *get* boils, of course, but that's because my body—my real body—is well nourished."

"Won't be by the time he's finished with it," Pete said.

"We'd better talk," I said.

"We are talking," said Angie.

"I mean about the body switch."

"Do we have to?"

"Yes, if we want to become ourselves again. We have to give the Toilet of Doom another flush."

"Toilet of Life," she corrected.

"Life? You call this life? Doom I said and Doom I meant."

"Whatever. You think another flush might reverse this?"

"Worth a try. Do you remember how you flushed away all the little people?" I asked Pete.

"Sure, why?"

"Well, it wasn't till all the little people had gone down all the little toilets that the big one with the 'F for Flush' invitation came up. So obviously you have to flush the little people again to give us another go at 'F for Flush.' Right?"

"What's in it for me?" he said.

"What do you mean, what's in it for you? You're our bud, Three Musketeers, one for all and all for lunch."

"This is business. Toilet business. Come on, what are you offering?"

"Will this do?" Angie said, raising one of my fists.

Pete jumped out of his chair—"Have to catch me first!"—and scooted up the tree we sat under.

"Like that's a *problem?*" Angie said, and scooted up after him.

He was out of his mind if he thought he could escape Angie just by climbing a tree. She's always been better at tree climbing than us. Been doing it since diapers. Pete and I used to watch her from our strollers, saying,

"Goo-ga-goo-ga, shouldn't that be us up there?" And she was even better at it in my body, for some reason. They'd both vanished into the leaves, which were shaking like crazy, and Pete was yelling like he'd just met a tree vampire—but not for long. The leaves parted and down he came. *Thludd!* It wasn't a long drop but he fell awkwardly, which made him a bit slow getting up. Too slow. Angie dropped on him and Pete squawked like a parrot about to be stuffed, rolled on his side, pulled his knees into his chest, and crossed his arms over his head half a second before she started pummeling him.

I leaned back in my bolted iron chair, smiling. The sun was out, there was a bit of a breeze, birds gargled, and one of my best friends was being beaten up by my other best friend. All I needed was a glass of something with bubbles from the café that never opened, half a dozen straws to slurp through, and my life would have been complete. I felt amazingly calm. Never felt so calm in my life. But that wasn't all. Everything looked so much brighter than usual. More interesting somehow. I don't think I ever looked at a tree or a bush before and thought, Hey, cool tree, cool bush. I did today, though. And the smells. The grass, the air, the things with petals. Terrific. Why hadn't I smelled them before? Was this what it was like for real girls? If so, all I can say is no wonder most of them are quieter in class and not thumping one another all the time and hassling the teachers.

After a while Angie got fed up with pummeling someone who didn't fight back and let Pete up. He was puffing a bit.

"I've lost a button," he said.

"Lucky that was all," said Angie.

They slumped back in their seats facing the bushes.

"Do you mind if I say something, Ange?" I said gently.

She glared at me. "Depends what."

"Well, you're a bit . . . um . . . violent today."

"Violent?"

"Yes. I mean you always had a temper, but—"

"Temper?" she said, folding my hands into fists. "Whaddayamean *temper*?!"

"Angela," I said. "A warthog with a bad home life has a better temper than you, even on your good days."

She aimed a swipe at me for the third time in an hour.

"See?" I said.

Surprisingly, she did. And all the anger and aggression immediately drained out of her.

"You're right," she said. "Ever since I got this miserable excuse for a body I've felt . . . tense. Hands keep balling up into fists and wanting to bash things. You know what it is, don't you?"

"No, what?"

"Testosterone."

"The chocolate bar?"

"Testosterone, you dork, not Toblerone."

"Teswotterone?" said Pete.

"Testosserone," I told him.

"You don't have any idea what it is, do you?" Angie said. I shrugged. She looked amazed: "Don't you two pay attention in *any* classes?"

"Try not to," said Pete.

"I'm talking human biology," she said. "I'm talking hormones."

"I know about hormones," I said. "Stallone has them."

"Stallone?"

"Yeah. Dad says that if he didn't have so many hormones he wouldn't be half as vicious and mean."

"Your dad?" said Pete.

"Stallone. They drive the old cat mental. You know when the hormones are buzzing because his tail shoots up like a radio antenna and suddenly he's flying up and down the room smacking walls—*smack! smack! smack!*—and all you can do is keep your head down. Terrifying."

"You want to get back to testosterone?" Angie said.

"Didn't know we'd left it."

"I'd better spell it out for you, seeing as you're so dim. Testosterone is something that—"

"You didn't spell it," Pete said. "You said you'd spell it out."

Angie ground my teeth to powder and started again. "Testosterone, in moron terms, is something males have a lot of and females don't."

"Like football and detentions," I said to Pete.

"Something *inside* them," Angie said. "Something that makes them want to fight all the time and disrupt class. Makes them crazy about fast cars and martial-arts videos. Makes them *violent*."

"I'm not like that," I said.

"You can be a pain in class."

"Naturally, I'm only human, but not the other stuff. Fast cars, martial arts, violence. I was never into any of that."

"That's because you're a wimp," she said.

"No, no. It's my hormones. Make me jig about instead, that's all."

"You're not jigging now," Pete said.

"The jig seems to go with the body, and that's out on loan. Only it doesn't make you jig," I said to Angie. "Makes you want to slug people."

She stood up suddenly and started pacing up and down. As she paced, her hands—my hands—kept folding into fists, and every few steps she forced them to unfold, then a few steps later they folded again.

"I can't help myself," she said. "God, I'd love a good fight right now!"

"Keep away from me," Pete said.

"I said *good* fight." She stopped pacing. Stared helplessly at us. "I think I'm turning into a psychopath."

"You could be right," I said. "Much longer on my testosserstuff and who knows what sort of monster you'll turn into."

"The Brook Farm residents'll be forming a posse to track you down and lead you away in chains," Pete said.

"Throw you into the deepest darkest dungeon till the flesh drops off my bones," I added.

Angie shook herself. Became all businesslike. "We have to reflush the Toilet of Doom and get our bodies back! Right away!"

"That's what I was saying a while ago."

"Yeah, well now I'm saying it, so let's get to it."

"We don't know it'll work," I pointed out calmly.

"No, but it's all there is. We've got to try!"

"If it doesn't we could be stuck like this," I said, still calm. "Then what?"

"Then one day soon Angie orders her first martial-arts video," Pete said, "and you accompany her mom to the bra shop."

I stopped being calm. I leaped up. So did Angie. We raced neck and neck for the park gates. Got home a good twenty minutes before Pete ambled in wiping tears of joy from his eyes.

10

We stood nervously behind Pete while he called up the Toilet of Life. The door with the sign on it appeared. Angie hadn't seen this, but Pete and I knew that when you clicked the sign the door opened on the toilet with the handle, and when you clicked the handle the screenful of smaller toilets came up, with all the little people walking around them, and when you flushed all the little people . . .

Except that today the sign on the door didn't say VACANT. It said OCCUPIED. Pete clicked it anyway.

The door didn't open.

He clicked again. Still didn't.

Angie grabbed his shoulder and hoisted him out of the chair. She took his place, clicked OCCUPIED. The door stayed shut. She clicked again. Still shut. And again. Still.

"We seem to have a teensy-weensy problem," I said.

"Oh, you give up too easily!"

She clicked OCCUPIED another five hundred times, furiously at first, less furiously, and slower and slower, as she realized she wasn't getting anywhere. Then she sat back, staring at the closed door, chewing my lip.

No one said anything for a while. Then Pete made a suggestion.

"Milo said he knows the guy who invented it. Maybe he could put us in touch with him. The inventor of the thing's bound to know how to get the door open."

"It's a thought," I said.

"A very good thought," said Pete, patting himself on the back with a ruler.

We'd never phoned the Dakin house before. If Milo's father had been someone else we might have had the number, but he wasn't, so we didn't. They were in the book, though, along with three other Dakins.

"Four Dakin households," I said. "Isn't one enough?"

"One more than enough," said Pete.

"Give me your cell," Angie said to him.

He wasn't happy about this. Nobody uses Pete's cell phone except him. Angie snatched it from him and buttoned the number.

"What if Face-Ache answers?" I said.

"I ask for Milo, what do you think?"

But Face-Ache didn't answer.

"Milo?" Angie said into the mouthpiece. "It's Angie."

"Jiggy," I said.

"Jiggy," she said. "Listen, Milo, question. You know that game you mentioned the other day, the Toilet of Doom?"

"Life," said Pete.

"Toilet of Life," she said. "Remember telling us about that?"

We put our ears close to the receiver so we could hear his reply.

"Funny you should mention that," Milo said. "I was talking to Mr. . . . my friend who invented it. . . . I was talking to him about it only yesterday. Well, he brought it up actually, and . . . Hey, you haven't been fooling with it, have you?"

"We took a look out of curiosity. Couldn't get the toilet door open."

"Oh, that'll be the glitch."

"The glitch?"

"My friend says it's not working the way it should. It jams, then suddenly starts up again and goes rogue."

"Rogue? What does that mean?"

"Doesn't do what it's supposed to. It started out as an ordinary game, he says, but it's proving a bit too clever for its own good. Said I'd better not mess with it until he's sorted it out. You'd better not either."

"Us?" Angie said, scowling at me. "No chance. Got more sense."

"Look, Jig, I can't talk now," Milo said. "My dad's really rattling me. Know what he's doing now? Ironing his shoelaces. I don't think I can handle this anymore."

He hung up. We all looked at the receiver.

There was a pause. Then Angie and I sank to the floor to await the end of the world. Pete didn't join us. His world was still going strong. He threw himself on the bed, put his arms under his head, smiled at the ceiling.

"I can't wait for tomorrow," he said.

"Why, what happens tomorrow?" I said.

"School."

"Oh. Yes. School."

I hadn't given school a thought until now. I don't on weekends if I can help it. But I gave it one now. Quite a big one. And groaned.

"Be a laugh," Pete said. "For me anyway. Not so much for you two. 'Specially Jiggy."

"Why 'specially me?"

"Well, you'll be the one in the skirt."

"Skirt?" I said. "Whoa. No. Not me."

"Girls have to wear the skirt uniform at Ranting Lane, it's the rules," Angie said.

"Yeah, but I'm not a girl. Not really."

"You look like one."

"But I'm not, that's the point."

"No, that *is* the point," she said. "You look like a girl, so you have to dress like one. It's the way it works."

"But even the skirt's not the best part," Pete said cheerfully.

"There's *more*?" I wailed.

"Oh yes!" he sang. "Oh yes, yes, *yes*! What day is it tomorrow?"

"Monday, why?"

"What do we do Monday afternoons?"

"Monday aftern . . . ?"

I realized. On Monday afternoons the boys play soccer with Mr. Rice and the girls do other things with Ms. Weeks. I glanced at Angie, expecting her to be as horrified as me. But she seemed to have perked up a bit.

"Soccer with Rice," she mused. "Could be veeery interesting."

"Oh yes," I said. "Right. I was forgetting. Just what you've always wanted, isn't it? Free license to kick boys where it hurts, elbow their ribs to extinction, shove their faces in the mud. But what about me? Do you realize what I'll have to wear *then*?"

"Yep," Pete said, picturing it all.

I'd probably have been pretty amused too if he'd been in my position. But he wasn't. It was me and me alone who was going to have to wear little green undies and a mini gym skirt.

"I'm taking tomorrow off," I said.

"You can't," Angie said. "If you don't go to school they'll think it's me not going."

"They can think what they like."

"You're going to school tomorrow if I have to drag you by the hair and stuff you into my gym clothes personally."

"You sound like my mother," I said. "You *look* more like my father, but you sound like my mother."

"Look at it as a challenge," Pete said. "I mean, how often do you get to do something like this?"

"Play field hockey in green undies? Hmm, tough one."

"Basketball tomorrow, not hockey," Angie said.

"Oh, happy day."

"Anyway, this body-swap thing could have worn off by morning. Maybe we'll wake up as ourselves."

"And maybe we won't."

"Even if we don't, it still might not last much longer. We could be back in the right bodies before first period tomorrow."

"Great," I said. "There we are in science and suddenly I'm myself again—in a girl's school uniform."

"I won't be able to sleep tonight," Pete said. "The way it's looking, tomorrow's going to be the highlight of my entire school career."

There was only one thing that made life worth living just then: the thought that I wouldn't have to do my detention tomorrow. Angie would have to do it for me. I didn't mention this. Not yet. It wasn't much, but I needed *something* to look forward to.

11

Now that Angie and I were supposed to be each other we had to swap houses. And rooms. And beds. The only reasonable thing about this for me was that Angie hates girlie stuff. I would have screamed myself to sleep if I'd had to jog to Dreamland in a frilly nightie. Still, frilly nightie or no frilly nightie, as I was turning in that night I fell to my knees and prayed to the great toilet in the sky to flush my body back to me while I slept. You may not be surprised to hear that when I woke up next morning and found for the umpteenth time that prayers don't work—mine anyway—I did not fling the comforter back with a hearty cheer and start hanging party balloons.

To avoid being caught doing something un-Angie by the resident Golden Oldies, I kept out of their way as much as possible that morning. I managed to miss them altogether by being slow going down. Audrey yelled that I'd be late for the last time as she and Oliver set off for work. "I'm coming, I'm coming!" I yelled back, but hung about upstairs until the front door closed.

When I went down I wore Angie's bathrobe over her school uniform. Pete was in the kitchen stuffing himself with Chocolate Cheerios in chocolate milk with a chocolate bar crumbled on top. Pete loves chocolate, can't get enough. And I'm the one who gets zits.

"Cold?" he said, seeing the robe.

"Nervous," I replied.

By the time we left for school I'd gotten a little more used to my new outfit but I still opened the front door like I expected the world's paparazzi to be there in force.

"Don't forget this," Pete said.

Angie's sports bag dangled from his fingers. I snatched it off him.

"Hey, what do I call you?" he said as we crossed the road.

"Call me?"

"Well, I can't call you Jiggy. Not in public. Have to be Angie."

"Call me Angie just once and you're a chalk outline on the blacktop."

We reached the opposite sidewalk. I looked at my ex-house. My house is called "The Dorks" and it's my fault, but I'm not going into that here.* I paused. How could I walk up that path, ring that plastic bell, wait patiently for my parents to open up and fail to recognize me as their son?

"I'll wait here," I said.

"Be bold!" said Pete, and lugged me up the path. He pressed the bell. "Hair looks nice," he said as we stood side by side on the step.

The door was opened by my mother. Dad stood behind her looking sorry for himself, hands on hips to give his armpits room to breathe.

"Hi, Pete. Hi, Angie," said Mom.

Pete grunted, like he does. Not me, though. I speak when spoken to.

"Hi, Mom. Hello, Dad."

My mother's eyebrows somersaulted over the back of her head.

"Twit," Pete said quietly.

"No," I said hastily. "No, I mean 'Hi, Peg. Hi, Mel.'"

Mom clawed her eyebrows back and smiled.

"Mom-Dad, Peg-Mel, what does it matter? We've all

---

* For the full pathetic story read our first so-called adventure, *The Poltergoose.*

known one another so long we're like one big happy family now."

"*Happy?*" my father cried, flinging his hands at the ceiling. "Have you seen my *armpits*?!"

"Oh, it's you two," a cranky voice said from above.

Angie clumped down the stairs in everything that was mine, including my school uniform and hair. My backpack and gym bag clumped after her. The Boil was so big and bright today you could see it from the door without focusing. When she made it to the hall, my mother kissed her on top of the head. And here's a funny thing. I hate being kissed by my mother in front of other people, but when she kissed Angie I felt a bit jealous. I mean she's my mother and she's kissing another kid. Yes, I know it was my head her lips were decorating with saliva, but I wasn't wearing it at the time, so . . .

"See you later," she said to Angie. "Have a good day, Musketeers!"

She went into the kitchen. Dad followed her, hands on hips.

"Still each other, then," I said as we sloped down the path. Angie didn't answer. I looked at her closely, avoiding the Boil, which believe me wasn't easy. "Angie, why are my eyes so red? What have you been doing to them? Hey, you haven't been crying?"

"No I have not!" she said. "If you must know, the free extra attachment got stuck in your zipper!"

"Ouch," said Pete.

"Takes a little practice," I said.

"I don't *want* to practice!" she said, and marched off.

We caught up to her. "My room to your liking?" I asked. "My pajamas?"

"Your pajamas were disgusting. Full of earth or something, went straight in the laundry basket. Your sheets weren't much better. But worst of all . . ." She shuddered. "Worst of all, I had to clean your *teeth.*"

"My house is your house, my teeth are your teeth."

"With *your* toothbrush!" she added.

"So what are you complaining about? You want to clean my teeth with *your* toothbrush?"

We'd almost made it off the estate, Angie walking a few steps in front with my boiled nose in the air, when . . .

"Hey, you three!"

We stepped aside to let Atkins through. He thwacked Pete's ankle with one of his bags, said "Hey, Ange!" to me, and scooted on to catch up with Angie herself.

"Hey, Jig," I heard him say. She snarled at him. Eejit peered at the Boil. "Ya wanna do somethin' about that, dude. Could turn toxic."

Angie didn't thank him for his kind advice. She gripped his scrawny neck, lifted him off the ground, and carried him along while he gasped for breath and kicked like a small person who just dived into a toilet.

"PUT THAT BOY DOWN, McCUE!" roared a deep voice.

"I didn't touch him!" I cried, spinning around with my hands up.

Ms. Weeks and Mr. Rice, our PE teachers, jogged by, him in his stupid red tracksuit, her in her nice green one. Ms. Weeks smiled, thinking I was fooling around, and even Rice didn't look quite as mean as usual, probably because he was with her.

"If you want to sue for assault, Atkins," Rice said, "we'll gladly be witnesses for the prosecution!"

Angie dropped Eejit's neck and he scampered after the happy joggers, wormed his way between them for protection, and tried to match them jog for jog. Interesting sight. Mr. Rice jogs like he's king of the world instead of a very tall jerk in a red tracksuit, and Ms. Weeks jogs like some golden-haired princess testing her new sneakers on a trampoline. Atkins jogged between them like a pet monkey in a school uniform.

We have to go through the shopping center to get

to school. Angie was still a little ahead of us, so she reached it first. A kid with green hair and a dog leaned out of a doorway and shoved a magazine in her face.

"*Fat Chance!* Help the homeless! *Fat Chance!*"

"Aw, help yourself!" Angie said, and slapped the magazine out of his hand.

The *Fat Chance* seller shrank back into the doorway until she was halfway across the square. So did the dog.

I felt a worry coming on. Dangerous combination, Angie's temper and my testoblerone. I could see it now. She bursts into the staff room during break, head-butts every teacher in sight, the Toilet of Doom thing wears off, we get our rightful bodies back, and next morning I'm standing in front of a firing squad in assembly.

"We have to do something," I said to Pete. "We have to make the Toilet of Doom work and get my body back while it's still in one piece."

"We tried," he said. "Door wouldn't open. Might never open again."

I grabbed him by the shoulders, put Angie's nose against his.

"There must be a way! We have to find it!"

"Go on, Garrett, give 'er a kiss," said Ryan, strolling by with Elvis Bisley.

Elvis laughed. Pete didn't. He shook me off.

"What are you trying to do to me? This'll be all around school by homeroom!"

Then he threw himself at Ryan and set about proving he didn't go in for all that sappy stuff. Watching them make mincemeat of each other, I suddenly felt very lonely. Very out of things.

12

You know it's weird, being a girl. The teachers and most of the other kids—even the boys—talk to you differently. Sort of gentler. Doesn't seem natural if you're not used to it. But there was one person who didn't seem to want to talk to me at all. When I walked in the classroom and sat in Angie's seat at the front, Julia Frame turned her back.

"Hey, Julia, how's tricks?"

"Huh!" she said.

"You're not still miffed about yesterday, are you? I was just kidding around, thought you'd know."

"It was a joke?" she said, half turning.

"'Course. I was all set to let you in on it and have a big laugh with you when you zonked out of there." I pasted a big phony smile on Angie's chops. "You didn't think I was *serious,* did you?"

"You really didn't mean it?"

"Not a word, Jools. Not a syllable. Not even a comma."

It did the job. Too well. She gave a great big sob of relief, threw her arms around me, and squeezed so hard I almost burst.

"What's all this?"

I looked up. Face-Ache Dakin stood over us. I ducked out of the Frame armlock. "Practicing self-defense, sir," I said, and made some hacking moves at her neck so he'd get the idea.

"Well, on your own time, please. This is a classroom, not a gym."

He went to his desk, told us to settle down, settle down, and started calling attendance. Calling names in alphabetical order must set Dakin up for the day. He calls the boys by their last names and the girls by their first *and* last, which seems pretty sexist to me. Even calls Milo by his last name.*

"Julia Frame!" he said when he got to her.

"Here," she said sulkily. She was half facing the other way again.

"Now what have I done?" I whispered over her shoulder.

* Not today, though. Didn't call him anything. Milo wasn't there.

96

"You pushed me off and hacked my neck," she whispered back.

"I had to," I said. "Dakin had come in, and—"

"Quiet, you two."

"Yes, sir. Dakin had come in," I repeated, "and he's not big on the huggy stuff. If he hadn't come in we could've hugged all day, no prob, but there you go."

She turned to face me again. She looked like she wanted to believe me. "Apologize, then."

I sighed. Did I have to go through this every time I opened Angie's mouth? Well, if it helped me blend into the background . . .

"Okay, but no more bear hugs in class. I'm sorry I pushed and hacked you. All right? That cover it? Now can we just sit here and enjoy attendance with our favorite teacher?"

"McCue!" said Face-Ache.

"Here!" I said.

The class stopped talking. Every eye swiveled my way.

"I said McCue, Angela, not Mint."

"Oh yeah, right, sorry, sir, wasn't paying attention."

"That's quite an admission for someone in my class."

"Thanks."

"McCue!" he said again.

This time I let Angie handle it. Then he said her name, which comes right after mine, and I answered again. Not one eyelid batted.

Most days, including Mondays, we don't have class with Face-Ache after attendance, so the second it's over we head for the door. Naturally we make as much noise as we can on the way, and naturally he screams and threatens us with every step—but not today. Today when we kicked our chairs back and charged we didn't get a peep out of him.

Outside, our mob headed for the science lab and crashed immediately into two other classes going in different directions. No one wanted to give way, of course, which meant there were arms and elbows and backpacks everywhere. For a minute it looked like there was going to be a riot. But then Mr. Rice's sweet little voice was heard:

"GET TO YOUR CLASSES, YOU PEOPLE, AND STOP ALL THIS NOISE!!!"

"He's quiet today," Angie said as we went on our way.

"Rice?" I said. "Quiet? Have you been shoveling wax into my ears?"

"I mean Dakin."

"Yeah, I noticed that," Pete said. "Spooky, I thought."

"Almost a different person," Angie said.

"Like he hired a whole new personality from the New Personality Shop," Pete said.

"Hey," I said.

"Hey what?" they said.

"Maybe Face-Ache's been Toilet of Dooming too."

We stopped in our tracks, eyes like marbles.

"Yeah," Pete said, "but to switch bodies there has to be someone else there, and Milo says they don't get visitors."

"Maybe they didn't need visitors," I said. "Maybe *they* switched."

"Are you saying it wasn't Dakin the Father taking attendance but Dakin the *Son*?" Angie said.

"It would explain why Milo wasn't in class."

"No. Couldn't happen. If Dakin woke up and discovered he'd turned into Milo overnight he'd have a heart attack."

"That's it!" (This was Pete in case you wonder.) "Face-Ache has a heart attack and Milo leaves him twitching on the floor. 'Free at last!' he thinks, sprinting for school in his father's body."

Angie shook her head. "Milo's a young kid in the prime of life and his dad's a dried-up old stick insect. If you were Milo, would you leap at the chance to wear a bag of bones like that?"

"Besides," I said, "if Milo took attendance there'd be telltale signs. Milo signs. No, that was Face-Ache all right. Bit quiet today, that's all."

"Don't look around," said Pete. "Think we're being followed."

Angie and I looked around. By this time we were the last of our class in the corridor. Last but one. Julia was still there. Trailing after us. After me.

"Think you've got yourself a fan," Angie said.

"Only because she thinks I'm you."

"No. Because you're being nice to her. Nicer than I am."

It was during morning break that Angie and I had to use the wrong school toilets for the first time. We'd put it off as long as possible, but couldn't hold it in any longer. We were standing in the corridor between the Boys' Room and the Girls' Room. No one had gone in or come out of either of them for a while but we still hung back. It's a big thing, using the opposite team's toilets.

"Go on then," Angie said.

"After you," I said.

"What's the big deal? All stalls in the Girls' Room. No one'll see."

"Be bold, Jig," said Pete.

"Will you stop saying that?" I said.

"And don't hang around in there," said Angie, shoving me at the door.

"Hang around? This'll be the fastest pee in history."

I was about to go in when Mr. Heathcliff, the janitor, arrived. Mr. Heathcliff has to be the most depressed person on the planet. He shuffled around the corner, paused, and looked me up and down, as if to say he knew all about me and was thinking of selling the story to the tabloids.

"Hi, Mr. Heathcliff," I said brightly.

"Er-*rum!*" said Heathcliff, which is all he ever seems to say, and shuffled by.

I threw the door back and shot in. A girl's gotta do what a girl's gotta do, even when she isn't one. I ran into a stall, bolted the door, dropped the fire-damaged underpants, and . . . well, you know the rest. Twenty seconds later I was washing Angie's hands and checking her hair in the mirror. Then I went out—and collided with four girls coming in.

"You were supposed to stop people," I said to Pete and Angie outside.

"We tried," said Pete.

"We failed," said Angie.

I let it go. It was Angie's turn.

"No one comes in," she said. "But no one. Right?"

She went into the Boys' Room. Pete and I stood to attention outside. And of course a batch of boys came along right away. One of them was my archenemy Bryan Ryan. Only today he didn't know he was my archenemy.

"What's up, Minty?" he said when I blocked his way.

"Can't go in."

"Why not?"

"Teachers' orders. Flooded. Have to use the Girls'."

"You're kidding."

"Would I kid you, Bry-Ry?"

"Well, what do the girls use?"

"The Teachers'."

"So what do the teachers use?"

"The Boys'."

"Oh."

They went into the Girls' Room. Pete and I legged it around the corner. We heard the screams and yells. Peeked back just in time to see Ryan and his pals shoot out again, ducking flying toilet-paper rolls.

13

The hardest part about being a girl at school isn't the classes, it's remembering to sit with your legs together when you're wearing a skirt. But even this was nothing compared to gym that Monday afternoon. Things were getting kind of tricky before we even left the locker room. I didn't know where to look when the girls started to get into their gym clothes, so I glued my eyes to the ceiling. They thought I was playing the fool. Thought I was playing it even more when I put my gym suit on. The green undies and skirt are worn over ordinary underwear, but I wasn't wearing ordinary underwear. I was wearing fire-damaged briefs (boys).

There was one last thing to put on when we were all decked out in our sporty skirts and undies. A bib. Yes, a bib. I never knew they were called that until now. Angie had kept it pretty quiet and I don't blame her.

"Why bibs, Ms. Weeks?" I asked. "I mean, what do you think we're going to do, drool yogurt suddenly?"

"Very funny, Angela."

Ms. Weeks hadn't gotten changed in the same room as us, of course, but she wore the same natty little green outfit—except for the bib. Probably felt she'd gotten her drooling pretty much under control by the age of almost thirty. As we filed out, I noticed Julia Frame trying to get near me and shoved Jodie Duthie and Jodie Gold between us. She looked kind of upset.

The soccer field is over to the right as you go down from the locker rooms. The boys were swarming toward it, yelling, rolling over, belting one another, while we girls walked to the basketball court in a quiet, orderly fashion. I don't think I ever felt so stupid in my life. I mean I might have looked like a girl, but I wasn't, not really. In my head I was a boy in a short skirt, green undies, and bib. Someone wolf-whistled from the soccer field. I didn't need to look to know who.

The basketball court has a high wire fence all around it, like a big cage. Ms. Weeks opened the gate and we trooped in. Then she stuck her arms out like a scarecrow.

"Red team that end, blue team that!"

"Which am I, Ms. Weeks?" I asked.

"Look at your chest, Angela."

"Why, what's wrong with it?"

"Your bib, don't be silly."

I looked at the bib on Angie's chest. It was a red one (bib, not chest). About half the girls wore red bibs, the rest wore blue ones. Some of the red girls were going one way and some of the blues were going the other, while a few of each stayed where they were, in the middle. I thought I'd better stick to the middle too and hope for the best. I gazed through the wire fence. Felt like a prisoner in there. I was, in a way. Over on the soccer field some of the boys were banging balls around and tripping one another up and Mr. Rice was screaming, "Hegarty, Sprinz, stop fighting!" Never speaks in a normal voice, old Rice Krispies. For the first time ever I wished I was over there with them, about to play soccer.

Something large and shapeless climbed into the corner of my eye. Julia Frame. I was starting to understand what Angie had against her. I ran across the court to get as far away from her as possible. I glanced back. She wasn't following.

"What are you doing over there, Angela?" Ms. Weeks shouted. "In position, please."

"I have a position?" I shouted back.

She didn't answer, just threw another arm out. I followed the arm until I came to Megan Larkin.

"Megan, what's my position? Must have gotten sunstroke yesterday. Can't remember stuff."

She frowned. Megan does a lot of frowning when I'm around, though usually when I'm in my own body. She's always telling me to grow up and all.

"Sunstroke?" she said. "It wasn't that sunny yesterday."

"It wasn't? Well, I said I don't remember stuff. Where do I go?"

"Look at your bib."

I glanced at Angie's chest again. "Looking."

"It says 'F'. That means you're a forward. You stand near the basket. You throw the ball into it." She sounded very suspicious as she said all this.

"Thanks," I said. "Buy you a glass of water sometime."

I sauntered toward my basket. So I was a forward. Cool. Sounded important. While I was strolling to the net I heard Rice screaming orders over on the soccer field.

"Divide yourselves into two teams by your last initial! A's to M's this side of the line, N's to Z's that side! Come on, move it, move it!"

A few boys ambled over the line one way or the other, but the rest just stood there scratching their heads.

"What do you mean last initial, sir?"

It was Pete. I frowned. It should have been me over there annoying Mr. Rice. Annoying Mr. Rice is one of those things I do really well.

"What do I mean?!" Rice bawled. "I mean the first letter of your last name, boy, what *else* could I mean?!"

"Oh, right." Pete glanced my way, then said, in an especially loud voice so I wouldn't miss it: "So if my name was, say, *McCue,* my initial would be M, right? It wouldn't be, say, B for Big Soft Girl?"

I leaped at the fence, fingers like claws in the holes. "I'll get you for that, Garrett, you snot-eyed relic!"

Just then I heard a voice in the distance. My voice.

"It's all right, Jig! I mean Angie! I'll do it!"

I dropped off the fence as Angie, in my body and soccer gear, put my head down and started toward Pete like a blind bull. Pete saw her coming, spun around, headed for the edge of the field.

"Where are you going, Garrett?!" Rice bawled.

Pete didn't answer. Or stop. Rice tried a different approach.

"Set one shoe off this field and you'll be cleaning the mud off mine for the rest of term!"

Now if there's one thing Pete hates, I mean really *hates,* it's cleaning things. You just have to look at his feet to know that. So he took a sharp right at the edge of the field and started along another side. Which meant that all Angie had to do was change direction and take a shortcut.

"And what do you think *you're* up to, McCue?!" Rice screamed.

Angie didn't answer either. A few more steps and she gave a mighty roar, made a flying leap, folded my arms around Pete's legs, and introduced his face to the worms. Then she jumped astride his back and grabbed his hair. I don't know what she planned to do next because Rice got there too soon and hauled her off. But he wasn't purple with rage like he usually is when catching one kid pulping another. Not a bit of it.

"That was some tackle, McCue! Perhaps you have hidden talents! Let's double-check, shall we? Ryan!!!"

Ryan ran up. Ryan will do anything to please Rice, the creep.

"Sir?"

"Run up to my office and grab a football!"

"Why do you want a football, sir? We're playing soccer."

"Change of plan! McCue just made the best tackle I've seen from a boy in years! I want to find out if he can do it again! Speed o' light, lad, speed o' light! Everyone else, switch fields!"

Ryan scowled—he's crazy about soccer, not football—and headed for the locker rooms, while Mr. Rice marched toward the football field. The boys watched him go. When he got there Rice turned, saw that he was alone, and gently asked the boys to please be kind enough to join him.

"GETYERBACKSIDESOVEREREYAUSELESS BUNCHABUMS!"

"All set, Angela?"

I looked around. "Do you mind if I just watch today, Ms. Weeks? Think I've twisted my ankle."

I limped bravely around in a little circle to prove it.

"You weren't limping just now."

"Trying not to, I hate missing basketball, but it's so painful."

"Just do your best. Right, girls, let's get cracking!"

So I played girls' basketball for the first time in my life. It wasn't too different from the boys' version, except for one thing. I was good at it. No. Better than good. I was a natural. Perhaps it was Angie's body, but even without my jigginess I was so fast on her feet that the world was a blur. When the ball came my way, all I had to do was reach out and I was holding it. Then all I had to do was stand on tiptoe, make a sharp upward movement with my borrowed elbows, and the ball was dropping through the net and my team was cheering and Ms. Weeks was saying, "Well done, Angela. You *have* improved suddenly!"

Yes, at last I'd found a sport I could do. And one I

enjoyed. But talk about Murphy's Law. Have you heard of Murphy's Law? Murphy was this ancient Irish saint who wrong things kept happening to. Whenever Saint Murphy prayed for stuff to happen it didn't, and whenever he prayed that it wouldn't it did. This became known as Murphy's Law, and it works pretty well for people who aren't saints too, especially if their name's McCue. Like until that day I'd never liked basketball, and suddenly I discover that basketball and me are made for each other. The Murphy's Law part was that the only way I'd be able to stay good at it was if I remained a girl.

Every now and then while I was being brilliant at shooting hoops I glanced across at the football field to see how they were getting on. There was one kid who looked like he wanted to make a name for himself. He did a lot of weaving in and out with the ball pinned to his chest, this kid. A lot of elbowing and shouldering people who got in the way. A lot of flying through the air and leg-grabbing so the owners of the legs nose-dived into the daisies. After a while anyone who had any sense headed the other way when he came near. I would have too, if I'd been there. He was terrifying.

And who was this warrior of the weird-shaped ball? Angie. In my body. Shattering for all time my carefully built-up reputation as an utterly useless athlete.

14

If you're a boy at Ranting Lane you have to strip after gym and get in the showers with all the other boys. I hate that, but I would have hated it even more if I'd had to shower with the girls. Fortunately the girls don't have to take showers if they don't want to, so I just got dressed again with my eyes on the ceiling, wishing girls wouldn't keep coming up to me in towels to say things like, "Hey, Angie, didn't know you were such a whiz at basketball. Can I be on your team next time?" Julia kept looking at me with pride, like she'd coached me personally or something. I gave her the celebrity wave a couple of times, then cut her out of my will.

I wondered how Angie was getting on. Mr. Rice never lets anyone out of showers unless they have a fake doctor's note from their computer, like Pete, so she would have to shower with the boys. Or so I thought. Should have learned by now never to underestimate the Mint. I waited for her and Pete to come out of the locker room. Pete had mopped most of the dirt off his face, but Angie hadn't bothered. There was mud on my face and neck, in my hair, my ears, under my nails, you name it, there was mud there. Even the Boil was all muddy, though I was glad to see she'd managed not to burst it. I asked her how she'd gotten out of showers.

"Told Rice I had a rash someplace private," she said.

"That wouldn't work with Rice."

"Ah, but Angie's the flavor of the day," Pete said. "You never saw the old Ricebag so pleased. Says she's a real find. As a football player."

I turned away to hide my misery. Because of what Angie had done today, Rice would expect the same sort of performance from me when I got my body back. My only consolation was that next time she donned the little green undies and bib, Angie would also find herself the star of a sport *she* hates.

Gym is the last period on Monday, so we headed for the gates with everyone else. But then I remembered.

"Whoa! Back up. Detention! Dakin!"

"Curses, forgot that," said Pete.

"Ah well, can't be helped. See you later."

"Where are you going?" Angie said.

"Home. Your home. Garrett and McCue have detentions, not Angie Mint."

"What? Oh *no!*"

"Better clean yourself up though, Ange. Face-Ache won't be too thrilled when you turn up looking like that."

She said something nasty and stormed back into school. Pete followed. It's the first time I've ever seen him head for detention laughing.

When I reached the estate I found something happening in the street between our houses. Barriers had been put up around a man pickaxing a hole while three others watched.

"Buried treasure?" I said. They didn't seem amused.

I went indoors and straight up to Pete's room. I turned on his PC, called up the Toilet of Life with a beating heart. The door with the sign appeared. It still read OCCUPIED. I clicked about insanely for a while, hoping enough clicks would wear it down, force it to become vacant. Didn't work.

Later, when Pete came in, he had two bits of news. The first was that Bryan Ryan had skipped detention (no surprise there). The second was that Milo Dakin had disappeared.

"Face-Ache said his bed wasn't slept in last night. He must have gone out after we phoned and not come back."

"Wow."

"I've never seen Dakin like that," he said. "All twitchy, not strict at all. Didn't even give us any work, just talked."

"About Milo?"

"No, about the women's dart championships in Outer Mongolia. Of course about Milo." He rubbed his hands with glee. "Think about it, Jig. There could be a house-to-house search. Doors kicked in. Tracker dogs up the stairs. We could be thrown into chairs and blinded by spotlights, everything we say taken down and used against us." His eyes lit up. "If Milo's found in a ditch we might even be on *TV*!"

I shook my head at him. "I just don't believe you sometimes."

"Yeah," he said, eyes still lit, "but on *TV* . . ."

15

For dinner that day, Angie's favorite was put in front of me. Spinach lasagna. I'm not a big fan of lasagna even when it doesn't look like cat puke.

"What's wrong with it?" Audrey asked when she saw me pushing it around the plate.

"You tell me," I said.

"What a waste. I paid good money for that. You eat too much after school, I'm always telling you."

It was like being at home. Only the names had been changed. And the faces and furniture.

After dinner—after I'd washed the dishes (it was Angie's turn on their rotten rotation)—Pete and I left the house. The hole was still in the road. The man who'd been digging it, and the three men who hadn't, sat together in the front of their van. Digging Man was tucking into a pizza he'd just had delivered. The other three were watching. Must have been trainees.

"Remember, you have different parents now," Pete said as we approached The Dorks.

"After that lasagna how could I forget?" I said.

Once again my mom opened the door. She's usually quickest off the mark when the doorbell rings. She didn't look in the best of moods.

"Hi, Peg." I was getting good at this. "Jiggy in?"

"In his room. Go on up."

"Thanks, Mom."

We went upstairs.

"Don't you knock?" Angie said as we barged in.

"Since when do I have to knock on my own door?" I said.

"That door is no longer yours. Keep checking the mirror, you'll get it eventually."

It was then that I noticed there was something different about the place.

"Angie, what . . . what have you done?"

"I tidied things up."

"Tidied things up? It's like I was never here. Never put my personal stamp on it."

"Yes, it's quite an improvement."

"And what are all these cushions doing?"

"They're cushions, what do you want them to do?"

"I mean what are they doing *here?* And so many. You breeding them or something?"

They were everywhere you looked, about three thousand of them.

"I like cushions," she said.

"If you like them so much why are there only two in your room? Your real room across the road. Where you sleep. Where you *belong.*"

"We don't have a cushion surplus. Stacks here, though. Your mom likes cushions too. Says you and your dad are always taking the stuffing out of her and her cushions, so she buys them and puts them away for a rainy day."

"Cushions won't keep much rain off," Pete said, stretching his arms out and belly-flopping onto a pile of them.

"Apart from the big cushion invasion," I said, trying not to look at them, "what's new at The Dorks?"

"Well, your mother's not speaking to your dad," Angie said.

"So what's *new* at The Dorks?"

"Oh, but this is really serious. She's furious about him taking Stallone to the vet behind her back."

"Why does she have a vet behind her back?" Pete said from the cushions. Pathetic.

"You mean he actually went through with it?" I said to Angie. "I thought it was just a heat-of-the-moment threat and he'd get over it."

"No. He took the morning off work 'specially. He told me everything while hiding from your mom. How he put on these extra-thick lumberjack gloves and snuck up on Stallone while he was eating the jellied pigeon brains he'd bought from the deli to distract him. How he put a rope around his neck and dragged him squealing into the dead-budgie cage."

"Stallone's too big to go through the door of the dead-budgie cage," I said.

"Your dad was up half the night turning one side into a door with a catch."

"And it held? Amazing. Whatever my dad's good at it isn't do-it-yourself. So he had the mad beast done. Poor old Stallone. How's he taking it?"

"He's not. He broke out of the cage in the waiting room. Hasn't been seen since."

"Like Milo," said Pete.

"Milo wasn't about to be snipped," I reminded him.

"We don't know that."

Angie said: "Maybe we ought to go and look for him."

"Who," I said. "Milo or Stallone?"

"I meant Stallone, but we could make it a double

search. Soon as we've checked to see if the Toilet of Doom's still occupied."

"It is. I took a look while you two were in detention."

"That was then," she said. "From what Milo said there's no telling when it'll work next, so we're going to check it again."

We yanked Pete out of the cushions and went downstairs. We left the house, started across the road.

"Stallone!" I cried suddenly.

"It's no good shouting for him," Angie said.

"No, I just saw him. Look!"

He sat under a lamppost some way along, one leg in the air. He'd been licking this leg when I shouted his name and it was still up there, drying out, when we started toward him. It wasn't until we got within hissing distance that he lowered the leg and ran around the corner on it and three others.

"Scaredy cat," said Pete.

"I wonder why he's still hanging around if he's left home?" Angie said.

"Nowhere else to go," I said.

"Maybe we should go after him."

"We'd never catch him. He'll come home when he's ready. Or not."

We turned back. The four workmen were at their

hole again. As we drew near there was a great roar and the man who'd been doing the pickaxing and pizza-eating started shaking himself silly with one of those big deafening road drills. The other three wore ear-muffs and watched.

Pete's room overlooks the street, so the drill was still pretty loud up there, even with the window closed. Angie pushed him into his swivel chair and told him to call up the Toilet of Doom. He did. And this time . . .

"Told you it was worth trying," Angie said.

"Click it, Pete, click it," I said excitedly.

Pete clicked the VACANT sign and the door swung open. And there it was, with the graffiti on the wall behind it.

The Toilet of Life
A Manx Game

"What now?" Angie said.

"He clicks the little handle on the side," I told her. "Go on, Pete, click the handle before it freezes again."

"I was going to."

He clicked the little handle. It moved, there was a flushing sound, and the toilet was immediately replaced by the screenful of much smaller toilets and little walking people.

"Get flushing!" I said.

"Will you stop giving me orders?" he said as one of the little toilet seats flew up. A little person gave a yelp and dived in, legs wriggling. There was a small flush and he slithered all the way down.

Angie and I looked at each other with shining eyes. It was going to happen! We were in with a chance of getting our bodies back!

Pete set to work. Soon little people were yelping and diving and getting flushed all over the screen.

And then they were gone. All of them. The screen changed. And we were looking at the Toilet of Life itself, and the immortal words:

Feel that your life has gone down the toilet?
Well, here's your chance to swap it
for a better one! Invite someone in who's
really got it made, hit "F for Flush," and . . .

Angie and I slapped hands in the air.

At the very instant we slapped hands the drill out in the street stopped. It stopped because the workman and his watchers had drilled through a power cable. All the electricity on our side of the estate went off. Pete's screen went blank.

And stayed that way until way past bedtime.

16

First thing in the morning I went to Pete's room and activated his computer. He raised his bleary head from the pillow.

"What are you doing?"

"Checking to see if the T of D's still vacant."

It was. But there was no point going to the next stage because Angie wasn't there. She had to be there when we hit "F for Flush" or I might find I'd swapped her body for something even worse, like a cockroach.

We'd arranged to meet for school half an hour earlier that morning. We hadn't had a chance to look for Milo last night and wanted to see if he'd returned home. The street was quiet when Pete and I left the house. The electricity vandal and his watchers hadn't arrived yet for another bash at their hole. Angie came out of The Dorks as we reached it. The Boil was starting to fester. Looked like it was getting all set to blow. I put Pete between us.

On the way to Milo's, Angie updated me on life at home. Mom still wasn't talking to Dad because Stallone was still missing.

"She sent your dad out to look for him last night. He was gone for hours, no sign. Peg says he'll be doing the same thing tonight and every night until Stallone's found either purring at the top of his voice or flattened by a Mack truck."

When we got to Pizzle End Road we lurked behind a tree near Milo's and waited for someone to come out. The only one who did was Face-Ache. They never go to school together, so this told us nothing. His walk did, though. All stooped and tragic like he was really suffering. Still, we had to make sure. When Dakin was well on his way we opened the gate and rapped the supershiny brass knocker for a couple of minutes. Nothing rapped back.

"Tracker dogs," said Pete as we left.

"Where?" I said.

He rubbed his hands together. "Anytime now."

We were approaching Mr. Mann's bus shelter and

the luxury apartment building opposite. Guys in white gloves and brand-new overalls were carrying furniture in from a moving van.*

"My dad gets really worked up about that place," Pete said.

"Mr. Mann's bus shelter?" said Angie.

"The luxury apartment building. Gets right up his snout that some people have that sort of money while he only has one car, six neckties, and a ballpoint pen."

"Wonder who owns them?" I said.

"My dad," said Pete.

"No, the apartments. The building."

"No one knows," Angie said. "The owner's anonymous."

"I know that. What I'm saying is, why would someone who owns an apartment building want to keep it secret?"

"What's going on there?" said Pete.

Four big teenage boys stood over Mr. Mann, who'd just looked up from his paper to see what was in his light. One of the boys was Jolyon Atkins, Eejit Atkins's older brother. We keep out of Jolyon's way. Everyone keeps out of Jolyon's way. He has this barbed-wire

* Into the luxury apartment building, not the bus shelter.

tattoo around his neck and the four fingers of his left hand are tattooed with H.A.T.E. Morons who have H.A.T.E. tattooed on one hand usually have L.O.V.E. tattooed on the other. Not Jolyon. He has H.A.T.E. on both.

We crept closer to catch what Jolyon and his gang were saying to Mr. Mann. It went something like this:

"You's a bum, man. Why don'tcha bum around sum other place?"

"Yeah, we don't want your kind here."

"Nah. Get lost, scum."

"Yeah. Or we'll thump ya."

"Give ya hell."

"Yeah."

Mr. Mann took his glasses off, smiled, and said, "Take a seat, friends. Sit and chat awhile. You're welcome to share my paper. Tell me, what do you make of the latest from the Balkans?"

Jolyon's forehead slumped over his eyes. It was only a little forehead, so it didn't have far to go.

"You takin' the proverbial?"

Mr. Mann frowned kindly up at him. "Sorry? Proverbial what?"

Jolyon growled. "You think I'm thick, don'tcha?"

"No, not at all. Here, let's read the obituaries together."

Jolyon gripped Mr. Mann by the lapel of his old over-coat. The other three leered, made sandpapery noises with their tonsils, all set to enjoy themselves as Jolyon's spare hand folded and drew back.

But then: "Atkins, you lamebrained dork, put that bum down!"

It was my voice. My real voice. And it wasn't coming from me.

"What do you say we keep out of this?" I said to Angie out of the side of my mouth. "I'd kind of like that body to live to see another . . ."

But she was already stalking toward the bus shelter, where the bundle of bullet heads stood gaping at her in amazement.

"Wha'chu call me, McCue?" Jolyon said.

"Lamebrained dork," Angie said. "And I was being polite."

"He'll tear her to shreds!" I said to Pete. "Tear *my body* to shreds!"

"Don't worry," Pete said, "you won't feel a thing."

Now she was standing in front of Jolyon, glaring up at him. She was quite a bit smaller than him, even in my body, but she didn't seem afraid. Well, why should she? By the time she came around, the broken legs, cauli-flower ears, and black eyes would probably be back on me. While glaring up at Jolyon she unlocked his fingers from the tramp's lapel. Mr. Mann just sat there looking quietly amused.

"You know who you're messin' with?" Jolyon said.

"'Course," Angie replied. "I'm messin' with a creep. A twerp. I'm messin' with Jolyon Atkins, who has a prune for a brain."

I gulped. "No," I whispered. "Take it back, Ange, take it back."

She didn't take it back, and Jolyon's forehead dropped even further. Then he gave her a shove. On the shoulder. It was meant to be the first of many shoves and lots of other stuff besides. I knew it, Pete knew it, Jolyon's Merry Men knew it, even Mr. Mann probably knew it. The only one who didn't seem to know was Angie.

"Do that again and you'll make me angry," she said to Jolyon. "You wouldn't like me when I'm angry, Atkins."

And of course Jolyon did it again. Other shoulder this time. His cronies chuckled. This was gonna be *soooo* funny. They were still chuckling when a fist shot out and dotted Jolyon on the nose. It must have been quite a dot because Jolyon said something like "Uh?" and immediately sat down. He stared up at Angie in surprise for a few seconds, then his eyelids fell and his head slumped forward. And that was that.

The chuckling of the cronies stopped. Angie turned to them. "Anyone else?" They held their hands up, shook their heads. "Well, get him out of here, he makes this bus shelter look untidy."

Jolyon's slack-jawed chums slotted their mitts into his pits and dragged him off, facedown, the toes of his shoes scraping the pavement.

"Come on, Pete!" I said.

We reached the bus shelter three seconds later, panting for breath.

"You all right, Ange? It was all so quick, couldn't get here before! Did they hurt you? You want us to go after them and give 'em what for? Just say the word, Ange!"

"It's all right, everything's under control," she said quietly.

And then it all floated through my mind: the not-so-distant future when I'm back in my own body and Jolyon Atkins remembers what happened here today and comes looking for me with a sledgehammer.

I heard Mr. Mann's voice in the distance. "What's your name, son?"

I heard the reply. "Angie. I mean Jiggy. Jiggy McCue. This is Angie."

I felt a jab in the ribs. I nodded to back her up. "Yes, that's right."

"Well, Jiggy McCue," he said to her, "I'm not sure how I would have come out of that little encounter if you hadn't come along, but I'm in your debt. I'd like to give you something for your trouble, a reward of some sort." He paused, then spread his arms to take in all his worldly goods. "I'd *like* to, but as you see . . ."

"Forget it," Angie said. "Glad to be of help."

"Very kind of you," Mr. Mann said. "But if there's anything I can ever do for you, all you have to do is ask."

"Thanks." She turned to go. Then turned back. "Wait. There might be something. A friend of ours has disappeared. Milo Dakin, lives just up the road there."

"I know Milo," Mr. Mann said. "Good boy."

"Yes, well, he didn't go home on Sunday night and he wasn't at school yesterday. 'Course, he might turn up today, but if he doesn't . . ."

"You sound concerned."

"I am. We all are. Things haven't been all that great at home lately."

"It's just him and his dad these days," I said. "And Mr. Dakin's pretty strict."

"He's a fanatic," Pete said. "We should know, he's our homeroom teacher."

"So I was just wondering if you've seen him," Angie said.

Mr. Mann sucked his lip for a while, deep in thought and hair. Then he said: "I can tell you something. It's not much, but you must promise not to pass it on to a living soul."

I looked at the others. "You have our word."

"Well then, you may rest assured that Milo is safe and has a roof over his head."

"Has he told you that?" Angie said.

Mr. Mann looked away. "One hears things on the street."

"But you know where he is?"

"I can say no more. I won't break a confidence."

"But think of his dad," I said. "He's worried sick."

At this he threw his head back and his great thick mane flew about his shoulders. A tiny lodger left his beard in a hurry.

"From what I've heard, a little worry wouldn't do that gentleman any harm. Might make him realize what he could lose if he doesn't start behaving more like a father, less like Franco."

"The hairdresser?" said Pete.

"The dictator. Now what happened to my paper . . . ?"

His paper had fallen on the ground. I scooped it up and handed it to him. He gave a bristly smile. His teeth looked like they hadn't been cleaned since the middle of the last century.

"I'd be lost without my morning paper. Mr. Murdoch the news agent very kindly brings it to me every morning—free of charge."

"You must know it by heart," Pete said.

We went on to school.

17

The first thing we saw after fighting our way through the school gates was a big notice on a board. Standing beside the board was our depressed janitor, Mr. Heathcliff.

"'Morning, Mr. Heathcliff," I said.

"Er-*rum,*" he said, and pointed at the notice.

The notice said that all pupils must go to the auditorium right after attendance. No hints what for, so there were a few worried looks. We only go to the auditorium once a week, for assembly, and assembly wasn't today. It could mean anything.

"Thanks a lot, Mr. Heathcliff," I said as the bell went.

"Er-*rum.*"

"I don't know why you bother to talk to that miserable specimen," Pete said on the way to class.

"Oh, I enjoy our little chats," I said.

Not only was Milo not in class again, but his old man wasn't either. Ms. Weeks was waiting for us instead.

"Where's Face-Ache, Ms. Weeks?" Pete asked.

"Who?"

"Dakin. Mister. Where?"

"Mr. Dakin's around. You'll see him shortly."

"Oh goody."

When she called the attendance she missed Milo completely. It was as if he'd ceased to exist. The moment she finished—even before we could kick our chairs over and race for the door—she stood up and smiled.

"Neil Downey, come to the front, please."

"Who me?" said Downey in surprise.

"Yes, Neil, you. The rest of you stay seated."

Downey slouched to the front, where Ms. Weeks turned his shoulders around to face the class.

"The attendance sheet informs me that it's Neil's birthday today. How about 'Happy Birthday to You,' everyone?"

"Happy birthday to you," we mumbled, and piled out. Downey isn't the most popular kid in the galaxy.

We joined the happy throng in the corridor and set off for the auditorium. Most of the school was there already, mumbling quietly. There was a row of chairs on the stage, with teachers on them looking serious— including Dakin, who looked even paler and tenser than usual.

"Worry," Angie said. "Maybe he's human after all."

"Maybe pigs have wheels," Pete said.

"Wings," I said.

"What?" he said.

"Pigs have wings," I said.

"Do they?" he said.

"No," I said.

"So why tell me they do?"

When the rest of the school had entered and sat down, Mr. Hubbard our principal came in with a policeman and a policewoman.

"Double strippergram for Downey's birthday?" Pete said.

It wasn't a double strippergram. Mother Hubbard introduced the couple in blue and they took turns, like they'd been rehearsing all night, to tell us about Milo's disappearance and ask us to come forward if we had any information or thoughts as to his whereabouts.

And that was it. We filed out again.

"What do we do?" I said.

"About what?" said Pete.

"Well, Mr. Mann seems to know where Milo is. We ought to tell."

"Can't," said Angie. "You gave him our word."

"Yeah, but this is serious. We could be arrested for withholding stuff. Criminal offense."

"They cut your hands off for that in Greece," Pete said.

"Greece?" I said.

"Well, somewhere."

"Also," Angie said, "if we squeal on Mr. Mann and they interrogate him and he tells everything he knows and they find Milo, they'll ask Milo why he left home, and it might come out that he has a lousy father, which could land Face-Ache in pretty hot water, maybe even lose him his job."

"That's true," said Pete.

He was halfway to the principal's office before we caught him and hauled him back.

First class of the day was geography. Our geography teacher, Mrs. Porterhouse, is very tiny and twice as skinny, with a voice like a bread knife. She isn't too bad most of the time, but every so often she does something she thinks will make geography more interesting. Some things are okay, like the field trips—trips to fields—but most are as boring as the back of Bryan Ryan's head. Recently Mrs. P. had been failing to get us interested in the people and customs of other lands, what they eat, what sort of houses or huts they live in, things like that.

Not exactly stirring stuff, but at least you could sleep through it. No dozing today, though. Today the crazy old bat was going to show us how they dance in Argentina. She was going to show us the tango. And make us dance it. With one another.

"Mrs. Porterhouse," I said as she led us into the gym where the sacrifice was to take place, "why don't we leave the Argentininians to do their own stupid dance and sit down quietly and look at their stamps instead?"

No dice. She slipped a CD into the little machine she'd brought with her.

"Now pay attention, everyone. The tango is a slow ballroom dance that . . ." The music started before she was ready. "Well, watch me." She started gliding and jerking around the gym like a grasshopper with a wooden leg. "You see? Looong gliding movements punctuated by ab-*rupt* pauses. Looong gliding movements punctuated by . . ."

It wouldn't have been quite so bad if we'd had to spend the class watching her make a fool of herself, but she wanted us to make fools of ourselves too. Pete realized how it was going to work even before I did and grabbed the nearest girl so he wouldn't get stuck with me. Kelly Ironmonger screamed and beat him off.

Pete held his hands out. "Anybody?"

There were no takers, but the Porterhouse took charge. "Susan, he's all yours."

Susan Berry's face screwed up like an old candy wrapper. "Dance with Garrett? Oh no. No, no, no, *no!*"

"He's no worse than the rest. And at least he's willing, unlike some."

"Some" meant every other boy there, who'd suddenly discovered their fingernails, the ceiling, the floor, and how not to whistle.

I caught Angie looking at me. When she saw that she'd gotten my full attention she gave me a cruel grin and skipped across the gym—yes, skipped, in *my* body!—and grabbed Laura Porritt by the hand. Laura tried to yank it back but Angie was too strong today and pulled her to her, body-to-body, face-to-face. Then she did a looong glide followed by an abrupt halt. Laura wailed miserably, but Angie kept her grip and did the same thing again, looong glide, abrupt halt, while Mrs. Porterhouse clapped. Yes clapped, silly woman.

"Well done, Jiggy, you've really got a feel for the tango!"

I turned to the wall and banged Angie's head slowly against it. In less than a minute my lifelong bud Angie Mint had killed my cool image stone dead. Boys would be talking about the day Jiggy McCue was praised for dancing the tango until they died laughing of old age.

I hung back as long as possible while partners were being chosen and rejected and forced on other kids, hoping that if I held out to the very end there'd be a boy shortage and I could spend the rest of the lesson sitting cross-legged on the floor doodling in the dust. I should be so lucky. When everyone else was paired off there was just me and one boy left. A boy no girl would dance with if he was the last one on Earth.

"Come on now, you two, don't be shy," Mrs. Porterhouse said. "Take hold of each other and let's get started."

I saw Pete cross his legs with delight as I gritted Angie's teeth and grabbed Eejit Atkins by the hand. Then I slung an arm around his waist and tested the looong glide.

"Angela, you're the girl," Porterhouse said. "The female. Ralph is the male and the male leads. He's the one who does the long glides. What you do is drape yourself around his leg and toss your hair."

I stared at the leg in question. "You want me to drape myself around *that*?"

"Oh, you can do it. See how well the others are doing? A couple of them anyway."

I didn't care how the others were doing. They were all trying to lead or not lead like the Argentinumians said they had to, but they didn't have Eejit Atkins's hand on their waist or have to drape themselves over his skanky leg. Still, I gave it my best shot. *Crash.*

"Hey, Wapshott, watch your stupid back! Who do you think you are—Zorro?"

As Atkins did a looong glide and twirled me over his leg out of time to the music, he said, "I never thought I'd be dancin' with you, Ange. Never in all my life."

It was then that I realized that Eejit had a thing for Angie. Such a thing did he have that he was grateful for anything he could get, even a scowl or a thick ear. I noticed Trevor Fisher trying to break Mariesa Knightingale's back over his knee, and an idea came to me. A way to get back at Angie for shattering my reputation here and on the sports field.

"Eejit," I said. "Ralph. Will you do me a favor?"

"Sure, Ange, what?"

"Well, I really hate the name Angie, and Angela's even worse. So I was thinking, seeing as we're dancing partners now, why don't you call me something else? Something personal. Just between ourselves when there's no one else around. A sort of . . . pet name."

"Pet name? You mean like . . . Fido?"

I bit Angie's tongue to stop it exploding.

"No, Ralph, I do not mean a dog's name, I mean something soft, gentle, like, well . . . Sweet Lips."

Even Atkins found this a tad hard to swallow.

"You want me to call you . . . Sweet Lips?"

"Keep your voice down, creep, this is between you and me."

We did some more looong glides, abrupt halts, and leg draping while he thought this over. When he'd gotten it all straight in his little skull he said: "You got yourself a deal, Ange." He lowered his voice and winked. "I mean . . . Sweet Lips."

"But only when we're alone," I said. "If there's anyone else within earshot it's still Angie, right? Remember, or I'll smash your face in."

"Cool," he said, shooting a foot out and crippling Martin Skinner for the rest of the day.

Picturing Angie's face when Eejit Atkins called her Sweet Lips for the first time, I danced the rest of the lesson away like a girl possessed. Happiest I'd been since I lost my free extra attachment.

18

We were heading home after another hard day at school, where two of us had had to pretend to be each other while the third found it highly amusing. Turning the corner into the main square of the shopping center we jerked to a sudden halt. In the middle of the square there's this big old tree with a railing around it, and on the lowest and biggest branch sat . . . Stallone. He was scarfing what looked like bird chop suey. Stallone's as fond of fresh bird as Pete is of chocolate.

"What do we do?" I said.

"We talk to him," Angie said, and marched toward the tree. "Stallone! Here, boy, here!"

Stallone looked up from his bird and snarled. Angie tried again.

"It's all right, Stal, no one's going to hurt you."

"Meaaarrrgh," growled Stallone.

"I don't get it," she said as we joined her. "He usually comes to me. I wouldn't harm him, he knows that."

"You might not," I said, "but he thinks you're my father's son and he isn't taking any chances in case you want to cart him back to the fruit-and-nut shop. I don't blame him. I know what it's like to suddenly be without the family jewels."

"And I know what it's like to suddenly have them," Angie said. "You can take me to the vet anytime you like."

Just then Stallone noticed me. His ears went up and the last bit of bird went down. He picked his way to the end of the branch, dropped off, and ran to me, hissing at Angie as he passed. I stooped to stroke him, but as I touched him a shiver went through him, end to end, and his back arched. He must have sensed I wasn't who I looked like. He shot out a claw and—

"Ow! You little monster!"

I whipped out a handkerchief and dabbed Angie's hand as Stallone became a blur on the far side of the square.

I thought that would be the last we'd see of him that day, and I wouldn't have been sorry, but we came across him again a few minutes later as we were passing the park gates. This time he had company that wasn't in his jaws. Very unexpected company. He sat on the path some way into the park, and on a bench facing him was . . .

"Milo," Angie breathed as we skidded to a halt.

We peered through the tall black railings. They hadn't seen us, just sat there looking at each other, not saying a word, even a meow, like they were in telepathic communication or something.

"First time I ever saw Stallone friendly with a non-female," I said.

"Kindred spirits," Angie said. "Two unwanted waifs together."

"Stallone's wanted. Sort of."

"We'd better go and talk to him," she said.

"We tried that, and look what he did to your hand."

"I mean Milo."

She went through the gates. Pete and I followed. We seem to spend our entire lives following Angie.

"Hey, Milo!" she called with a cheery wave.

Milo jumped. He looked our way. So did Stallone. We strolled toward them. For a second neither of them moved, then Stallone's tail shot up and he scooted off like he'd been fired from a catapult. Milo didn't hang about either. Instead of returning the cheery wave he jumped up and also hightailed it.

"Ever get the feeling you're not wanted?" I said.

"All the time," said Pete.

We continued homeward. We went to The Dorks first so Angie could change out of my school things. Mom and Dad weren't home yet, so Pete and I dived into the cookie jar. Should have waited until Angie had gone upstairs. She forced me to drop the handful of Oreos I'd been about to cram into her mouth.

"I don't want zits and boils all over *my* body!" she said.

I moaned of course, but said, "Okay, I'll just nibble one," and waited until she went before stuffing even more in her face than I'd been planning to.

I was a bit nervous. I'd been thinking about the Toilet of Doom all day, on and off. What if the sign on the toilet door said OCCUPIED again? It might be weeks before it would let us in for a second flush. In no time at all Angie had made me a tango king and football star. I dreaded to think what she might turn me into if she had my body much longer.

When she'd changed we headed across the road. The workmen had gone. So had the hole, which they'd disguised with asphalt of a different shade. In the house we found Audrey Mint looking flustered in rolled-up jeans and a fancy head scarf. She looked like a fortune-teller who'd seen the future and didn't like it.

"Good day?" she said.

"Good day," we said, and started upstairs.

"Keep out of Pete's room," she called after us.

"Why?"

She pushed past us carrying a plastic basket of cleaning things.

"I'm giving it a good going-over. Vacuuming, dusting, polishing, removing all the candy-bar wrappers from under the bed. In fact generally making it habitable."

Pete scowled. "I like it unhabitable."

We went to Angie's room, where we took turns facing the other way while I changed out of her school uniform and Pete changed into the jeans and T-shirt Audrey threw out of his room for him. Then we went back to The Dorks and up to my ex-room. I wasn't going to admit it to Angie, but the six million cushions were starting to grow on me. Maybe I'd keep a few when I got my room back.

We sat around twiddling our toes for a while, feeling helpless. We needed to get to Pete's computer and couldn't. Frustrating. Eventually Angie told Pete to call her mom. He refused, so she slapped him around the back of the head and did it herself.

"How's Pete's room coming?" she said into the phone. She looked at us. "Slowly, she says."

Slowly she said and slowly she meant. Every half hour or so Angie called and the answer was always that it wasn't ready yet. Somewhere in all this my mom came home and offered to rustle up some french fries

and hot dogs. We didn't refuse. The fries were great—
she makes really terrific fries, my mom—though the
dogs could have been better. I mentioned this, forgetting that it wasn't my job to pick holes in her cooking.

"They're vegetarian," she said.

"But we're not," I said. "It's like chewing grilled
gerbil droppings."

"Very nutritious."

About half-past eight Angie phoned again. This time
the answer was: "Almost there. Five minutes."

We twiddled our toes for five more minutes, then
recrossed the road. Twenty-five minutes later we were
allowed into Pete's room, which was tidier than it had
ever been since he moved in, and even smelled good.
"It's lost everything!" he wailed, but we didn't give him
a chance to wallow in his misery. I turned the computer on and pushed him into his swivel chair.

"Toilet of Doom. Pronto."

19

Good news. The sign on the toilet door still said VACANT.

The door opened at a single click. Another click activated the toilet handle and brought up the screenful of baby toilets with the little people walking around them. Pete flushed the people in the wink of an eye, and up it came, the thing that had brought this upon Angie and me, the Toilet of Doom itself, with its quivering seat, and:

**Feel that your life has gone down the toilet?
Well, here's your chance to—**

"All yours," said Pete, vacating the swivel.

I glanced at Angie. She looked as edgy as I felt.

"It's got to work," I said. "I want my body back."

"Not half as much as I want mine back," she said. "Get on with it."

"Oh no," I said, "not me, not again. This time you can get the blame if it goes wrong."

She growled the way she does when you argue with her, but took her place at the PC.

"Wait till I'm gone," said Pete, sprinting to the door. He closed it firmly behind him.

"Ready?" Angie said to me.

"Not really," I said.

She hit "F for Flush."

And nothing happened.

"Maybe there's a knack," I said, "and you don't have it."

"I'm using your fingers."

"Could be an attitude thing."

"Are you criticizing my *attitude* now?" she said.

"Wouldn't dare."

She hit "F for Flush" again. Harder.

Still nothing.

"Work, darn it, work!" she said, and hit it again. And again. And again. Nothing happened each time and she got madder and madder.

"Looks like I'm going to have to do it after all," I said with a kindly smile.

"Over your dead body!" she said, and gave "F for Flush" such a belt it's a wonder it didn't turn into an "I."

But it worked. The quivering seat flew up and the

blue cloud shot out of the toilet and spread across the inside of the screen. We waited for the next bit with bated breath, whatever that is. It was still bated when the cloud started seeping into the room and, after a pause, went all sparkly.

"What's taking so long?" Pete said, opening the door.

The cloud reached out and hauled him in. The door closed behind him like it had been kicked by an invisible foot

"Well done, Pete," I said, clapping softly.

Then all the little sparkly bits started going *pop-pop-pop* and . . .

"We forgot about the smell!" Angie cried. "Why didn't you open the *window*?"

"Why didn't *you*?" I said.

It was hard to see through all the stinky blue sparkle but we set off toward where the door had been last time we looked—and smacked into Pete also trying to find it. There was a bit of a struggle and quite a lot of un-printable language, but we eventually made it to the landing. As we closed the door, the Toilet of Doom gave a hearty flush.

It was done. For better or worse, it was done.

Halfway downstairs we began to feel dizzy. All three of us. Pete flopped onto the sixth stair, or maybe it was the seventh, but Angie and I had done this before and managed to get all the way down. We yanked the front door open and stood gratefully sucking the air out of the night.

"Feeling groggy," she said.

"Me too. But listen, before we lose it: where do we sleep tonight?"

"Same as last night. 'Case we don't switch back."

"But if we do switch in our sleep I'll wake up as me in your room and you'll wake up as you in mine. How do we explain that to—?"

"What's going on?" said Oliver Garrett, looking out of the living room, where he was watching TV.

"Just going home," Angie said, and tottered off the step.

I shut the door. "What's up with him?" Oliver said, meaning Pete, who was snoring on the stairs, face jammed between the vertical bars.

"It's been a long day," I said. "We had dancing."

I crawled halfway up the stairs, grabbed Pete by the collar, and with a superhuman effort bumped him up to the top. I dropped him outside his room and opened the door—cautiously. The horrible smell was gone already and the blue cloud was shrinking back into the screen.

Then, before my sleepy eyes, the last of it tumbled into the little toilet, the seat fell, and the toilet vanished.

I dragged Pete into the room. Tried to get him on the bed but my strength was going, so I left him half on, half off and staggered to Angie's room. There I reached for her stars-and-planets pajamas, but after a bit of a fumble I gave up, crawled onto the bed as I was. Didn't even cover myself. Then I slept. This time if I dreamed I don't remember. Maybe I was too excited to dream. Or nervous. The moment of truth was just a night away.

I woke up feeling different. More human somehow. My heart thumped. But was it *my* heart? I felt my hair. It was short! I jumped off the bed. I dropped Angie's jeans. I gripped the band of my fire-damaged briefs. Looked inside. Tears sprang to my eyes. I was a boy again!

Creeaaak.

Someone outside the door. The sloppy grin flew off my face. Who? If it was Audrey or Oliver, what could I possibly say when they found me standing there in the wrong house, wrong bedroom, Angie's jeans around my ankles, gazing fondly into my underpants?

I tugged the jeans up and dived under the covers. I made a little peephole so I could see out but not be seen seeing. The door opened. A face looked in. Not Audrey's, though. Nor Oliver's. Not even Pete's. Someone else's entirely.

Mine.

I threw back the covers and sat on the side of the

bed, staring at the me in the doorway. What was going on? I'd checked the hardware, knew I wasn't Angie anymore, but how could I be in two places at once?

The other me came in, went silently to the dressing table, grabbed a little mirror, brought it to me. I looked into it. The face that stared back was not the one I expected. The one I longed to see. Far from it.

It was Pete's.

The phone on the landing rang. The person who looked like me—who hadn't said a word so far—went out, took the phone off the hook, and brought it inside.

"Hi, Ange," he said. "No, it's Pete. I don't sound like Pete? Now I wonder why that is. Hey, wait a minute, think I know. Must be something to do with"—he paused, then shouted—"THE COLOSSAL BOIL ON THE END OF MY STINKING ROTTEN NOSE!!!"

He clicked the phone off and drop-kicked it across the room. It rang again almost at once. I scampered to it, picked it up.

"Angie, it's me, Jiggy."

"Jiggy?" she said. "Are you sure?"

"Not really, no."

"Listen, if you two are pulling my whatsit . . ."

"Wish we were," I said miserably.

"So what do you think happened?"

"I can tell you exactly what happened. There was an extra person in the room. A person who shouldn't have been there. A person who left his brain on the landing and came in and RUINED EVERYTHING!"

I threw the phone at Pete. I'm pleased to say he didn't duck fast enough. What had I done to deserve this? If the T of Doom could only handle one switch at a time, why couldn't it have been me who got his rightful body back? Why couldn't Pete and Angie have switched? At least they could live in their own house.

The phone was still bouncing when it rang again. I snatched it up.

"What!"

"Something seems to be wrong with the phone," Angie said.

"At least it's still a phone!" I snapped.

"Look, we have to get the new show on the road. I need to get out of here before I'm seen. Bring me my school clothes. Clean ones. When you come over Pete can jump into yours and take my place here."

This time she hung up. I didn't look at the receiver. Didn't look at Pete either. I couldn't, any more than I could speak to him. I went to his room and climbed into his school clothes (all except the underpants) while he put on jeans and a sweater. I bundled a set of clean clothes for Angie down my shirt—Pete's shirt.

"Don't get yourself seen," I snarled. "You don't live here today."

"Thanks for telling me," he snarled back.

I went down first. He crept after me. Downstairs I looked in the kitchen. Audrey and Oliver were there. She was eating bran flakes and banana, he was frying eggs.

"Just going to see Jiggy for a minute. Back for breakfast."

"Don't tell me," Oliver said. "I'm not making it."

Pete had slipped out while this friendly chat was taking place. He crossed the road ahead of me. I didn't bother to catch up to him. I noticed that he was moving strangely, awkwardly, like a penguin. It was obvious what had happened. He'd got my jigginess and couldn't handle it. He reached The Dorks and rang the plastic bell. I joined him on the step. I took a sneaky gander at the Boil. It was pretty nasty. Huge and soft and oozy.

My father answered the door for a change. His arms were hanging more or less normally now, though I knew from his strained expression that Mom still hadn't let him off the hook about Stallone.

"Thought you were upstairs," he said to Pete.

"New health kick," Pete replied. "Early-morning jogs till my eighty-fifth birthday. If I don't keep it up stop my allowance for life."

Dad gave my bulging shirt a suspicious look, but let us in. We went up to my room. Angie was waiting for us, still in my clothes from the day before. It was strange seeing her face on her again. I'd just started to get used to wearing it myself.

She looked from one to the other of us. "This better not be your stupid idea of a joke. . . ."

"Joke?" I said. "Do you see me laughing?"

I opened Pete's shirt and Angie's scrunched-up clothes fell out.

"Well, thanks a lot," she said, picking them up and untangling them. She didn't say it through her teeth, though, like she would have done yesterday. And suddenly she was all smiles. "You have no idea how good it is to have your own body back!"

"That's right, rub it in," I said.

"And I feel so . . . *calm*. You know, all that testosterone can't be good for you. Now I know why there are so many wars. Men are basically violent. They can't help it. Have to prove they're the toughest bipeds on the block. Have to fight, or get others to do it for them.

Women ought to turn on them, round them up, put them all on a great big island in the middle of nothing, and burn the boats."

"Have you finished?" I said.

"I'm just getting warmed up," she said.

"Well later, eh? Things to do here."

"Give me those rotten clothes," Pete said to Angie.

"Turn the other way, then."

We looked at the wall while she got out of my clothes and put hers on.

"Where you going?" I said when Pete headed for the door with my things under my arm.

"Bathroom, d'you mind?"

"Don't give a monkey's what you do." When we were alone I said to Angie: "You know the worst thing about *this* switch?"

"Pete's feet?" she said.

"Pete's feet. Inside these socks are the filthiest plates in history. I could start a Great Plague by just wriggling the toes."

"Well, at least you won't have to put them in your bed."

"No," I wailed. "I'll have to put them in *his*!"

When Pete returned from the bathroom there was something different about him. Something else I mean.

"Garrett," I said. "You evil specimen. You mutant clone of a dung beetle. You . . . you . . ."

I ran out of insults. All I could think of was the state of my beloved face. Stare helplessly at the red-and-yellow lava streaming from the squashed mini-volcano on my nose.

Pete grinned. With my lips, my teeth. He said: "I've been wanting to do that for days."

21

Angie might have been glad to have her body back, but she wasn't so glad to be sitting next to Julia again. I wasn't all that happy sitting next to Pete either, especially as I had to sit in his seat and pretend to *be* him. When I was blamed for his useless homework I seriously thought of throttling him in public. The reason I didn't was that he was blamed for mine.

At first I kind of missed the big calm feeling that had come with Angie's carcass, but I soon got used to being without and it was kind of nice having all the right attachments back in place, even if they weren't my own. The only thing that wasn't so good was the lack of jigginess. All right, when I get agitated and start jerking around some people laugh, but that's okay. I wouldn't be me if I sat still the whole time. I mean I'm Jiggy McCue, I jig, it's what I do. I got quite envious when a couple of the teachers told Pete off for twitching while they talked. They thought he was acting up.

But we got through the morning, and by lunchtime Pete and I were just about talking again. We went with Angie to our private bench in the Concrete Garden and ate one another's chips and sandwiches like we always do. Julia Frame stood behind a nearby bush waiting to be noticed and invited to join us but we ignored her. Over in the playground Mr. Dakin was on whistle duty. He didn't whistle once, just wandered about in these tight little sorrowful circles while kids beat one another up all around him.

"I feel sorry for him," Angie said.

"Sorry for Face-Ache?" Pete said. "Have you been at the Dr Pepper again?"

"But look at him, he's so unhappy."

"Good."

She wheeled on him. "Have you no *heart*, Garrett?"

"Sure," he said. "Jiggy's."

She turned to me. "We've got to persuade Milo to go back home."

"But we like Milo," I reminded her.

"We still have to persuade him it's not safe for a kid out there."

"Have to catch him first. Don't forget, he runs from us."

"So we run faster. He's got to go home."

"Ah, there you are, McCue, looking for you every-where!" boomed a voice so loud and seriously macho that the Julia Frame bush squawked.

"Whatever it is I didn't do it," I said to Mr. Rice, my favorite X-Man.

"Not you, Garrett, McCue. Got some news for you!" he said to Pete.

"You're moving to another school as a lunch lady?" Pete said.

"No! You've volunteered for the school football team!"

"I didn't know we had a football team."

"We didn't! But after Monday, when you showed what you can do, I decided to put one together!"

"When I showed what I . . . ? Oh. Yeah." Pete grinned at Angie and me. "Good, wasn't I?"

"Didn't know you had it in you!" said the jolly red bozo. "Locker room, tomorrow lunchtime, full uniform!"

"Lunchtime?" Pete said. "No, no. Lunchtime's when lunch gets eaten. That's why it's called lunchtime. I know it's kind of hard to get your head around, sir, but give it a whirl, eh? Chip?"

"Never mind *lunch*, boy! Have you no *vision*?! This could be the making of you! Do well here and you could end up representing the nation in the Baghdad

Olympics! Lunchtime tomorrow, locker room, or I'll hunt you down like a mangy dog and use your bladder as a lampshade!"

The sad old headcase jogged away.

"Thanks, Ange," I said. "I always wanted to be Jock of the Year."

"Sorry, Jig. Got a bit carried away."

"You should worry," Pete said to me. "It's not you who'll be spending tomorrow lunchtime facedown in the mud."

"Oh yes it is," I said.

"It is?" he said hopefully.

"Yes. Because the first thing we do when we get home today is flush ourselves back into the right bodies."

"Not if the 'Occupied' sign's back we don't."

"Think positive," I said. "This time tomorrow I want you sitting here happily munching and slurping while I'm out there making mud pies and a fool of myself."

"Cool with me," said Pete.

Suddenly Angie jumped up and yelled at the bush she'd been ignoring so well.

"Julia Frame, will you leave me ALONE!!!"

The bush shook like it had been hit with a flame-thrower. Then there was a high-pitched sob, followed by the *plicker-placker-pluck* of Framish feet running into the distance. I'm glad to report I didn't feel a thing.

"Back to normal." Angie beamed. "Great!"

She managed to dump another admirer too before the day was done. We'd made it to the last bell without any major disasters and joined the scramble for the gates. Angie was a couple of kids ahead of us when Eejit Atkins slammed his backpack in the back of my legs and said "See ya, Jig" to Pete before running to catch up with Angie. He'd been sidling up to her all day, trying to get her on her own, but was frightened off by her scowl or raised hand. He obviously thought he was home free now that school was over, though, because he tugged her sleeve, stood on tiptoe, and whispered something in her ear.

"Watch this," I said to Pete.

Angie's head jerked back. She stared at Eejit in disbelief. She must have asked him to say it again because Atkins did a repeat performance. And she belted him.

We caught up with her. "What was that all about?" I asked innocently.

"Do you know what that little slimeball called me?" she said.

"No, what?"

It wasn't easy keeping a straight face, even Pete's, and I must have given myself away because her eyes glinted suddenly as she realized who must have put Eejit up to it.

"Hey, just a bit of fun," I said.

"Prepare to die, McCue."

I took a sudden right instead of left out of the gates and hoofed it.

"Another time, Sweet Lips!"

"You won't get far!" she shouted. "Not on those legs!"

She fought her way through the crowd and came after me. Pete followed, shouting "What's this all about?" He didn't get an answer.

I'd hardly gone a hundred yards before I started wheezing. Pete has about as much wind as a sixty-a-day smoker. And Angie was right about his legs. I just made it to Downmarket before they started to give way under me. I stopped, breathing hard, waiting for her to reach me and put my lights out, thanking my lucky stars that she no longer had my fists of steel. But by the time they caught up she wasn't really angry anymore. I think she even saw the funny side, though she wouldn't admit it. Just gave me a little clip around the ear.

"Haven't been here for a while," Pete said.

"Haven't missed much," I said, gasping like a trout out of water.

Downmarket used to be the town's main street, but since the new shopping center was built most people go there instead. Some of the Downmarket shops have gone out of business and a whole bunch of them were knocked down to make way for the apartment complex for filthy-rich people. The delivery entrance to the apartments is on the Downmarket side, but most of the windows face the other way so the filthy-rich people don't have to look at the wrong side of the tracks. I peered in the Laundromat where Mom used to take me and the week's washing before she got a machine of her own. Nothing had changed. Same ratty old machines. Same old notice to the customers:

AUTOMATIC WASHING MACHINES.
PLEASE REMOVE ALL YOUR CLOTHES
WHEN LIGHT GOES OUT.

We walked past the bombed-out drugstore, the vandalized deli, the little old repair shop where the lights never worked.

"*Fat Chance!* Help the homeless! Get your *Fat Chance* here!"

Angie's arm shot out and pinned Pete and me to a garbage can.

"Could that be who I think it is?" she said.

The *Fat Chance* seller stood outside the boarded-up

travel agent's with a magazine bag at his feet. He wasn't like most *Fat Chance* sellers. You don't often see one in a hairy red wig and wraparound sunglasses. And he didn't have a dog. He had a cat. And the cat was . . .

Yep. You've got it.

We went into huddled-whisper mode.

"You think it's him?" I said.

"Has to be," said Pete.

"Got to be careful how we handle this," Angie said.

"Yeah," we agreed.

"Delicately. With kid gloves."

"Absolutely."

We tiptoed from doorway to doorway until we were just one short of our quarry. Amazingly, Stallone, who has ears like a bat rather than a cat, didn't once look our way, just sat there staring at nothing like he was in Deep Thought. There was no one else about, no would-be customers, but it didn't seem to matter to the *Fat Chance* seller, who went right on yelling.

"*Fat Chance,* ladies and gentlemen! Help put a roof over someone's head! *Fat Chance! Fat Chance!*"

"Remember," Angie whispered. "Delicate. Kid gloves."

We nodded. And jumped him. Dragged him into the boarded-up travel agent's doorway.

Stallone didn't hang around while we ripped his new friend's wig and glasses off. Even Angie calling his name in her own voice didn't slow him down. Milo Dakin stared up at us from the ground.

"Jiggy? Pete? Angie?"

"That's us," I said. "Just don't ask who's who."

"Will you get off me, please?"

We got off him, but when he was on his feet Angie gripped his left wrist and I gripped his right wrist and Pete got down on one knee to grip both of his ankles.

"Why are you holding on to me?" he asked.

"Don't want you running off again," Angie said.

"I can run if I want. I like running."

"But why from us? We're your friends."

"I have some stuff to figure out. Need to be on my own."

"Talk to us, Milo," I said.

"Just keep it short," Pete said from the ground. "I'm usually at home by now stuffing myself in front of the tube."

"I'm not saying a word until you let go of me," Milo said. "Feel stupid standing here with you all hanging on my wrists and ankles like chains."

"We'll let go if you promise not to run again," Angie said.

"I promise, I promise."

We let go of him.

"What are you doing selling *Fat Chance* anyway?" I asked him.

"I have to eat. I get sixty percent of every copy I sell."

"Sixty percent of nothing won't fill you out much. No one buys *Fat Chance*."

"Well, I've sold twenty-nine today."

We all goggled in amazement.

"You sold twenty-nine copies of *Fat Chance*?" Pete said. "You got sixty percent of twenty-nine *Fat Chances*???"

"One more and I was going to knock off and go for a seafood kabob," Milo said.

I did a quick run-through of all the things regular loot like that could buy. "Milo, how does a person become a *Fat Chance* seller?"

"Well, in my case I know the guy who publishes it."

"The publisher of *Fat Chance* lives in our town? And you know him?"

"Yes. Yes."

"Wow. Wow."

"Don't you have to be sixteen or eighteen or something to sell things on the street?" Angie said.

"My friend's pretty laid-back about stuff like that," Milo said. "I had to try and look older, though, in case the law came along."

"The hairy red wig and wraparound sunglasses?" I said.

"Yeah. Pretty good, eh?"

"Had us fooled."

"So what gave me away?"

"Er . . ."

"The cat," Angie said. Milo looked puzzled. "Saw him with you in the park yesterday—remember?"

"Oh yeah, right." He smiled. "I keep bumping into him. Some stray, I guess. Good cat. Very gentle, very affectionate."

"Maybe Stallone's been Toilet of Dooming," I said quietly to Pete. "Swapped fur and tempers with a sweeter kitty."

"Not judging from the scar on Angie's hand," he said.

"Tell us why you ran away from home," Angie said to Milo.

"Nothing to tell," he replied. "I've left, is all."

"You can't leave home just like that," I said. "I mean I think about it all the time, but I don't *do* it. Worse places than home, Milo."

"Depends on the home."

"Your dad's really worried," Angie said.

He perked up a bit at this. "He is?"

"Going crazy," said Pete happily.

"Yeah?"

"The police are combing the country for you," I told him.

"They are?"

"Sky'll be full of helicopters and searchlights anytime now," said Pete, looking up.

"Cool."

"Where are you sleeping anyway?" Angie asked him. "Not in one of these doorways."

"No, not in a doorway."

"So where?"

Milo suddenly became sly. "Somewhere."

"Well obviously *somewhere*," Angie said. "*Where* is what I'm asking."

"How do I know you won't tell anyone?"

"Milo, it's us," I said. "We're on your side."

He thought for a minute. "All right," he said when the minute was up. "But you have to swear you won't tell anyone. I mean *anyone,* and when I say 'tell' that includes writing it down and drawing directions."

"It's a deal." I looked at the others. "Right?"

"Right," said Angie.

"Whatever," said Pete.

Milo picked up the wig and wraparounds and stuffed them in his magazine bag. He slung the bag over his shoulder.

"It's up here."

We parted to let him through but Angie and I crowded him all along the street so he couldn't change his mind and make a break for it. He didn't say much as he led us back the way we'd just come, but he kept giving Pete these looks. Pete wasn't even *trying* to be me, or perhaps he was doing it on purpose so Milo would think it was me twitching like a maniac and hopping along the curb like Long John Silver, one foot on, one off. Soon as I got the chance I'd have to tell him everything. Didn't like the idea of Milo thinking I'd become a moron overnight.

"Here we are," he said, stopping suddenly. We stopped

too. Seemed silly not to, seeing as we were supposed to be following him.

"This is the delivery entrance of the luxury apartments," Angie said.

Milo smiled and fished a key ring out of his pocket. There were two keys on it. He slotted one of them in the lock and opened the door.

"What is this?" I said.

"It's a door," he said. "An open one. Go through it. If people see us hanging around out here they'll think we're up to something."

We went in. At speed. Milo turned a light on and shut the door.

"Where did you get those keys?" Angie demanded.

"A friend."

"Popular all of a sudden, aren't you?" I said. "Who's this one?"

"You don't need to know."

There wasn't much to see. It was just a sort of hallway with a big plain elevator. No luxuries for delivery people.

"You sleep *here*?" Pete said.

"No, not here."

Milo thumbed the button to call the elevator. The doors swished open.

"Get in."

We weren't exactly delirious about this. Our friend and classmate Milo Dakin had keys to the apartment building that only filthy-rich people and delivery guys can enter, and we weren't either one. But we got in the elevator. Milo punched the top button on a vertical panel.

"You can't be sleeping on the roof," I said as the doors swished shut and the elevator shot up like a rocket.

"Almost," he said.

The lights on the panel winked on and off like fireflies and in no time it was stopping at the top floor and the doors were swishing open again. We stepped into a little hallway almost identical to the one at the bottom. It even had a door, except this one didn't open onto the street, which was probably just as well.

"Here?" Angie said.

"Almost," said Milo again.

He opened the door that didn't lead to the street. On the other side there was another little hallway, a much fancier one, with a couple of nice pictures on the wall and soft lighting, and a luxury carpet so thick it felt like quicksand. There was another elevator too, but this one had doors like mirrors. And that was it, apart from one final door. The final door was made of polished wood and on it there were two words.

PENTHOUSE SUITE

"Don't tell us," Pete said. "You live in the penthouse."

We had a really good laugh about that. We only stopped laughing when Milo stuck the second key in the penthouse door, opened it, and went in.

"What are you standing out there for?" he said.

We stepped into the penthouse like three little mice into some big old fat cat's luxury litter box. The door closed quietly behind us. Everything about the place was quiet. In the first room, the living room, there was a luxury couch and chairs, a luxury coffee table, luxury curtains and lampshades. We wandered into the other rooms, checked out the three luxury bedrooms, the luxury bathroom, luxury kitchen, luxury fridge magnets. It was a pretty luxurious place.

I went back to the living room ahead of the others. It was hard work trudging through carpets as thick as those without snowshoes, but I wanted to see the view from the luxury windows that ran all along one side of the room. I've lived in this town all my life but I never had a chance to see it from so high up before. And oh boy. I had no idea we lived in such a beautiful place. Even the crummy old Old Town below looked kind of nice from up there.

I heard Angie's voice, speaking in the luxury distance behind me.

"Don't you know you can be locked up for breaking into rich people's pads, Milo?"

"I didn't break in. You saw the keys."

"I saw them but I don't know where you got them and that's what worries me."

"I told you, they belong to a friend. He owns the place."

"Nobody owns these apartments," I said from the window. "They're rented out by this anonymous person, well-known fact."

"My friend's the anonymous person," Milo said.

"What?"

"He's letting me stay here because it isn't rented yet."

"Are you trying to tell us," Angie said slowly, "that as well as being all buddy-bud-buds with the publisher of *Fat Chance*, you're pals with the owner of a luxury building for the very wealthy?"

"Plus the evil genius who invented the Toilet of Life," said Pete. "Don't forget him."

"They're all the same person," said Milo.

"All the same . . . ?" I said, gaping.

"How come you know someone who does all those

things?" said Angie. She made it sound like an accusation.

"How does anyone know anyone?"

"Tell us about him."

He shifted from one foot to the other and back again. He looked uncomfortable. Well, it's not easy standing on one foot at a time.

"Better not. He likes to keep quiet about the personal stuff."

"Anything you tell us won't leave this room," Angie said. "I swear. On Pete's life."

"Is there anything to eat in this dump?" Pete said on cue.

"All right, I'll tell you," Milo said.

"Great," said Pete.

But Milo didn't mean him. "Some of it anyway. My friend started this computer games company and it made him rich. He had half a dozen cars, couple of fantastic homes, a stack of people working for him, and a wife and two kids he almost never saw."

"Why didn't he see the wife and kids?" Angie wanted to know.

"Too busy. Not enough hours in the day."

"Bet the wife didn't like that."

"Not a lot. She walked out on him."

"What about the kids?"

"They walked with her."

"I'd have left the kids and taken the silver," said Pete, poking about for food.

"It hit him hard," Milo said. "He sent her tickets for an all-expenses-paid trip to the Bahamas for one adult and two minors. Thought that after she'd spent some boring quality time on a long white beach with palm trees and hammocks she'd be glad to come back and they'd live happily ever after—until they got so old and doddering the kids had to put them in a home anyway."

"There must be *some* grub here," Pete said, still poking about. "Whoever heard of a luxury pad without *food*?"

"And did they?" Angie asked Milo. "Come back afterwards?"

"No. They might have, but . . ." He sighed sadly. "But the plane went down on the way there."

"Went down? You mean . . . ?"

"Everyone on board was killed."

"Oh," Angie said. There wasn't a lot else *to* say.

"He blamed himself," Milo said.

"Don't see why," said Pete, slamming a cupboard door. "He only bought three of the tickets."

"He almost went crazy. Sold the business, cars, houses, got rid of the staff. Vowed never again to care about his own comfort or do things for his own profit."

"He owns this building," Angie said. "He obviously didn't give everything up if he owns all this."

"He doesn't make anything out of this," Milo told her. "Hands over every penny he takes in rent to good causes."

"Anonymously," I said.

"Right."

"A real saint," said Pete, wandering through to the kitchen.

"What I don't understand," Angie said, "is why, if your pal owns all this and lets you stay here for nothing, you have to sell *Fat Chance* to make food money."

"He's providing a bed and shelter but I have to bring my own food in," Milo said. "It's his only condition. He doesn't believe in free rides."

"Okay. But who is he? What's his name, where does he live?"

Milo opened his mouth, maybe to tell us, maybe not, but before he could do either Pete bounded in from the kitchen with the biggest box of chocolates you ever saw.

"Now we're *cookin'*! Can I open this, Milo?"

"Help yourself. Some woman gave them to me in the street. Very big woman. Said *Fat Chance* made her feel guilty."

"Probably thought it was a slimming magazine," I said.

Pete ripped the lid off and dove in. I groaned. My body had just lost the worst boil of its career and now all this gunge was being shoveled into it. I mean I like the occasional chocolate, but Pete . . . Pete doesn't know where to stop.

"What's up, Milo?" I heard Angie say.

Milo had slumped onto the couch. He looked pretty gloomy.

"Ah, nothing. Well yes. I sort of . . . stupid I know . . . miss home."

"That's not stupid," Angie said.

"Yes it is," said Pete, stuffing my face.

"I mean it's nice enough here," Milo said. "I can do anything I like except scribble on the walls and swing from the lights, but . . . you know what? This'll kill you. When I moved in the other day I threw my stuff all over the place, and then, next morning . . ."

Angie sat down next to him. "You tidied up again."

"Put it all in alphabetical order."

"Sounds to me like you don't belong here. Be happier at home."

"Oh, I wouldn't say *happier*." But she'd hit the nail, you could tell.

"Your dad'll be glad to see you. He's been terrible since you left."

"He's always terrible."

"He's gone very quiet. Hasn't really told anyone off all week or handed out a single detention, far as I know. Walks around all by himself with his head down—like this."

She got up and did a New Face-Ache impression around the room.

"He walks like that?" Milo said.

"Only during break," said Pete, stuffing my face.

Angie had gotten to him. Really tweaked his heartstrings. For the next ten minutes she continued to pluck them mercilessly, saying how sad his father was, how she was sure he was a reformed character and all, until the tears were bouncing off Milo's cheeks like liquid confetti.

After that, it was just a matter of time before he was gathering up the duffel bags he'd brought from home and leading the way to the door. "Oops, almost forgot," he said, and went back for a thin gray case that stood against a wall. "My friend's laptop. Been looking after it for him. He asked me to take it to him tomorrow so he can shut down the toilet game."

"He runs the Toilet of Doo—Toilet of Life from that?" I said.

"Guess so. He doesn't have some high-tech office or anything."

"And he's going to shut it down?"

"So he says. Says it's turned out to be a scientific breakthrough we're not ready for. By this time tomorrow the Toilet of Life will be no more."

"No more . . ." I said faintly. Well that's it, I thought. I'm stewed. I'm going to be Pete Garrett, rotten feet and all, until the day his heart gives out.

Pete hadn't heard a word Milo said about the Toilet of Doom being shut down. Chocolate, that's all he was interested in. When we left the penthouse and hit the street the ginormous box of chocs were still with him. Halfway to Milo's he said: "Only the orange creams left. Don't like orange creams." He offered them around. We pulled faces. "Ah well."

While he forced himself to scarf the orange creams I pulled Angie back a bit. "I think we should tell him," I whispered.

"Tell Pete he's a pig?"

"Tell Milo about the body switch. Then he can ask his friend not to shut the T of D down until we've flushed ourselves back."

"This isn't the time," she said. "Look at his little face."

"What about his little face?"

"He's excited. He's trying not to show it, but I bet he hasn't felt this eager to go home since his mom left.

This is an important moment for him. We can't throw a whole new set of wrenches in his works."

"One wrench, that's all I'm asking, just one wrench. And all he has to do is pass it on to his pal."

"No," she said firmly. "We'll flush you and Pete back when we get home and that'll be an end of it."

"The 'Occupied' sign might be back by then."

"Chance we'll have to take."

"Funny how you're happy to take chances when it's not you that stands to lose your body forever, isn't it?" I said.

"And you," she retorted with a scowl, "could try thinking about someone *else* for a change."

She rejoined Milo and jollied him along all the way home so he wouldn't get depressed again and run back to the penthouse. Pete wasn't looking too well as we approached the Dakin residence, but he valiantly polished off the last orange cream and stuffed the box in an overcrowded trash can. It fell straight out again.

Reaching the gate we crouched behind Dakin's perfect hedge while Milo had an attack of nerves.

"He could blow his top when he sees me on the step," he said.

"He could," Angie said. "But you have to do this, Milo."

"Yeah. Guess I do."

He stood up and stuck his chest out. Lifted the catch on the gate.

"We'll stick around till you go in."

"Thanks, Ange," he said to her. "Thanks, Jig," he said to Pete. "Thanks, Pete," he said to me.

The gate clicked shut. He walked up the path and banged the shiny knocker. We watched and listened through the perfect little holes in the hedge. Saw the door open, super-slow, like it was being opened by a very old lady, or a hamster. Then there was Face-Ache on the WELCOME, WIPE YOUR FEET mat. But he was so different from the Face-Ache we knew and hated, sort of feeble and lost instead of fierce and tense. His hair was all over the place and his shoulders looked like they could use a coat hanger. The finishing touch, the cardigan and tartan slippers, made you want to call a suicide hotline.

"Hi, Dad," said Milo.

It could have gone either way. Dakin could have snapped to attention and started shouting, bundled Milo inside, and told him to vacuum the stairs and *do a good job*. But instead the old boy's jaw hit his chest, the sorrow on his mug switched to Instant Happiness, and he grabbed Milo and . . . hugged him. Yes, we actually saw Face-Ache Dakin in a full-frontal man-to-boy hug.

And while he was hugging he kissed the top of the poor kid's head, kissed it so many times I don't know why Milo didn't disintegrate in embarrassment.

"Touching," Angie whispered.

"Gets you right there," I whispered back.

"I feel sick," whispered Pete.

Then Dakin hauled Milo inside and the door closed behind them.

"How's that for a happy ending?" Angie said.

"Hard to beat," I said. "Now how about one for me? The one that has to happen tonight if I don't want to be tottering to the post office fifty years from now with a Social Security check made out to Pete Garrett."

Just then there was a sound to our right. It was like someone puking. We looked toward the sound. It was Pete. Puking. Into Face-Ache Dakin's perfect hedge.

I was all for going straight up to Pete's room when we got back, but Pete was too green around the gills and slunk off to my house for a lie-down.

"Probably just as well," Angie said. "I mean, what's the first thing that happens after the sparkly-stinky cloud hits you?"

"You want air."

"Yeah, but then what?"

"You want to go to sleep?"

"Right. And if both of you get sleepy before dinner the Golden Oldies will start asking questions. One thing we don't want is Golden Oldie questions. GOs are like dogs with bones once they get started, and before they're done, you've told them every secret you ever had and most of everyone else's."

"Okay. But it has to be tonight, I don't care how sick he is."

While waiting for Pete to get himself together I turned his computer on and called up the Toilet of Life. The VACANT sign was still on the door. I clicked on it to stop it flipping to OCCUPIED and shutting us out. The door opened on the toilet with the graffiti and handle. I clicked the handle, the toilet flushed, and the screenful of smaller toilets and people took its place. Of course, I needed Pete there before hitting "F for Flush" but I wanted to be ready for when he turned up, so I started clicking around to try and flush the little people away. I clicked everywhere but couldn't find the trigger that made them yelp and dive into the toilets. It was painful to admit it but I needed Pete even for that.

We gave him an hour or two to recover, then I started calling him. No answer for a while, but eventually the croaky voice of a very ancient person said, "Go away, I want to die," and he hung up. Angie snatched the phone and dialed again. This time she got in first when he picked up—with a threat to do something terrible to him if he didn't shift himself. Twenty minutes later Pete tottered over. As well as looking pretty rough he didn't look very happy. This was because he'd spent the ten minutes since he crawled downstairs being screamed at by my mother.

"Doesn't she go *on*?" he said to me. "You know your boil? You know I burst it?"

"Yeees . . . ?"

"Well, I thought I'd never hear the last of it. Nag, nag, nag. Mirror, mirror, mirror. Disgusting, disgusting, disgusting."

I forced him into the swivel chair.

"Get clicking."

He got clicking, but slower than usual, much slower, like every click hurt. Still, one after another the little people yelped, dived into the toilets, got flushed, and eventually the Toilet of Life came up with the banner inviting us to hit "F for Flush."

"Nothing must go wrong this time," I said to Pete. "This is our last flush. When I wake up in the morning I want to be back in my own body and no one else's."

"You're welcome to it. Your guts are killing me."

"Might be a good idea to open the window this time," Angie said. She went to it, opened it. "Neighborhood Catwatch is out," she said.

I joined her at the window. Across the road, my father was just leaving the house to start his nightly Stallone hunt. He was halfway along the street when a fast sleek shadow caught our eye.

"Speak of the devil," Angie said.

"Devil cat," I said.

Stallone, unnoticed by my dad, jumped onto the garage roof below Pete's window and stared up at us. The light caught his eyes. They were like burning coals, but green.

"Stalloo-one," Angie called softly. "Stalloo-one. Come to Angie. Come on, come to Angie now."

He didn't budge. Maybe he was thinking about it. Maybe he was trying to translate Angie's invitation into Catese. Maybe he was just plain thick.

"Do you two animal lovers mind if we get this over with?" Pete said. "I need to lie down again."

I headed for the computer. "Yeah, let's do it. Next time I see that face I want it to be in a mirror."

"Likewise," he said, and hit "F for Flush."

"Not yet!" I said. "Angie's still here!"

"Oh yeah. Sorry."

"He didn't," said Angie in disbelief.

"He did," I said as the toilet seat flipped up.

She darted toward the door, head down. "You jerk, Garrett. You think I want to be turned into one of you two losers again!?"

As the blue cloud spread across the screen, I heard another movement behind me. Stallone had decided to accept Angie's invite. She was just closing the door as he jumped in the window and tore after her—too late. *Slam. Thud.* Cat skull on wood.

"That's women for you, Stal," I said. "Make a fuss over you when it suits them, slam the door in your face the moment the toilet seat's up."

"Here it comes," Pete said as the blue cloud began to seep out of the screen. He got off his chair and backed away. "Do you think we should hold hands?"

"Not while this body has a pulse," I said.

So we stood side by side, waiting for the cloud to cover us and do its stuff. Soon we could hardly see for blue fog, and then the sparkly bits appeared and started going *pop-pop-pop,* and then . . . the horrible stink. We palmed our noses and staggered about wondering how long we had to put up with it for it to work. I caught a glimpse of Stallone trying to climb a curtain, but I had enough to think about without him. When we couldn't take any more, Pete and I groped for the door. We found it, then it was behind us, closed, and we were lurching downstairs supported by the banister.

Angie was waiting for us in the hall. She opened the front door seconds before we got to it. Pete and I leaned out for a bucket or two of oxygen. Then came the need to sleep. Pete didn't hang around. He headed across the road yawning my head off. "Perhaps I should go over there instead," I called after him, but if he heard he didn't let on.

I clawed my way upstairs. Opened Pete's bedroom door. The cloud was already shrinking back into the computer, its work done, and you could hardly smell a thing now except furniture polish. I started groggily for the bed, tripped over something: Stallone, who'd fallen off the curtain and passed out on the floor. I dropped onto the bed. I didn't care that Pete had slept in it. Didn't care about anything. A few hours from now I'd be myself again.

Wouldn't I?

Early. Very. A voice calling me. Quietly.

"Jiggy? Pete? Whichever you are, are you awake?"

A hand pinched my shoulder.

I lifted the pillow from my face and squinted up through half-closed lids, hoping they were my own.

And saw Angie's face crack in two.

"It worked!"

"Really? You're not kidding?"

But I knew she wasn't. I knew my own gorgeous voice when I heard it. She handed me a mirror. I looked into it. Kissed it. Oh, that beautiful burst boil! I was so happy I could even put up with the ache in my guts from all the chocolate Pete had shoved into them. I broke into song.

"Quiet! You're not supposed to be here."

I was about to continue singing more quietly when I caught a movement on the far side of the bed. I peered over.

It was Pete, lying curled up on the floor. He was just waking up.

"What are you doing here?" I said. "When did you come back, and what for?"

Angie came around and also looked. Pete stared up at us from the floor. He seemed quite puzzled himself. But then, all of a sudden, he jumped at Angie. She tumbled backward, and before she even hit the carpet he was licking her face.

"Pete, you pinhead, what the *hell!*"

She shoved him off. Got to her feet. But he wasn't finished with her yet. He started winding himself around her legs and . . . purring.

"Ange," I said.

"What?" she said.

"I don't think it's Pete."

"Uh? 'Course it's Pete. Just Pete being even more of a knucklebrain than usual."

"Look at him. Does Pete, even at his most knuckle-brained, do *that?*"

He was sprawling on the floor with his legs in the air, inviting her to tickle his belly.

Her hands slapped her cheeks.

"You mean . . . ?"

I nodded. "Stallone."

"But Stallone's a *cat.*"

"Right. And he was in the room with me and Pete when we flushed the T of D last night."

"No, he wasn't."

"Was. He snuck in through the window just as you left. Really put his nose out of joint that you weren't there anymore. Literally."

"But if this is Stallone in Pete's body . . ."

"Yes," I said. "What's in my room over the road?"

I went to the window. Across the street my mother had just come out for the morning paper. A small furry creature with four paws and a tail slipped out after her. A pair of underpants was tangled around one of his legs. He shook them off and hid behind a bush until Mom went back indoors. Then he sauntered to the edge of the sidewalk, looked left and right, and, when no traffic came, stood up on his hind legs and crossed the road. With his paws over his dangly bits.

When it was time to leave for school the three of us, all in the right uniforms for a change, detoured over Milo's way hoping to bump into him and see how things were at home. I felt fantastic. Not only did I have my body back at last, but I could hardly walk in a straight line, so jiggy was I. We were almost at Milo's when we saw him and his father closing their gate and setting off for school together. Must have been the first time ever. And you should have seen them. Face-Ache's hand rested on Milo's shoulder, and every now and then as they walked Milo looked up at him—and they smiled at each other.

"Never saw Face-Ache so happy," said Angie.

"It's no good," I said. "You can't have someone called Face-Ache being happy."

We followed them. At a distance. Didn't want to intrude. I noticed that as well as his backpack Milo carried a laptop-shaped bag.

"Why would he be taking the anonymous friend's laptop to school?" I said.

"Maybe the anonymous friend's a teacher," Angie said.

"A teacher? At Ranting Lane? Get real."

"Hey, what if it's Mr. Rice?"

I laughed. The thought of the big Rice Krispie being a secret Good Person who only wanted to help people . . . per-Rice-less!

As Milo and his old fella drew near Mr. Mann's bus shelter someone shuffled past us: a downtrodden, sorrowful soul I'd never seen out of school before.

I stopped. Stared. Suddenly everything fell into place.

"What's up with you?" Angie said.

"I know who it is, Ange."

I pointed at the downtrodden, sorrowful figure trudging miserably ahead of us.

"Heathcliff? You can't be serious. I mean he's so . . ."

"Anonymous? Right. Heathcliff is the most anonymous person in the universe. He lives in a broom closet without any comforts or luxuries except a little TV and three thousand dusters. What a cover! Wouldn't occur to anyone for a minute that our humble, depressed school janitor could also be someone who builds luxury apartments, publishes a magazine for the homeless, and invents dangerous interactive computer games. It's so *obvious* once you think of it!"

"You know," Angie said thoughtfully, "you might just be right."

"I *know* I am. Heathcliff's our man or my name's not Jiggy McCue."

We started walking again so as to keep Heathcliff, Milo, and Face-Ache in sight. Heathcliff surprised us a bit by suddenly shuffling into the road, but we decided he must be going to the filthy-rich apartment building.

"Wants to check everything's in good luxury running order," I said.

Heathcliff reached the opposite sidewalk just as Milo and Face-Ache drew level with Mr. Mann's bus shelter on our side. Milo grinned at Mr. Mann and gave him a thumbs-up. Mr. Mann grinned back and hoisted a thumb of his own. Then, without his father seeing, Milo slipped him the laptop. I glanced across the road. Heathcliff had shuffled past the apartment building and gone into the newsstand. You could have knocked me down with a pixel.

"What did you say your name was?" Angie said.

While I struggled to come to terms with this unexpected twist, a man stepped out of the luxury apartment building and crossed the road. It was the official-looking type we'd seen here before. He headed for the bus shelter and spoke to Mr. Mann.

"Let's give them a listen," Angie said.

We scooted around the back of the bus shelter, where Angie and I pressed our ears to the wood and the third Musketeer rolled into a ball and licked the front of his trousers.

"Check to sign," we heard the official-looking type say. "The donation to Kids in Need."

"It says fifty thousand," Mr. Mann said. "Wallace, I told you to make it out for a hundred."

"I'm supposed to be looking after your financial affairs," the Wallace guy replied. "I'm trying to stop you bankrupting yourself."

"Let me worry about that. Tear this up and make out another—for a hundred grand."

Wallace sighed disapprovingly. "Well you're the boss."

"Remember that," said Mr. Mann. "What's the latest on the apartments?"

"Just three still to be rented—not counting the penthouse."

"You can put the penthouse back on the market. My young friend who was using it doesn't need it anymore. Oh, and there's a *Fat Chance* opening. Scout around for another homeless person who wants to work."

"Yes, Mr. Mann."

Angie and I slipped out from hiding and hit the sidewalk on the far side of the bus shelter.

"Wait!" she said. "We're one short!"

She dashed back for the third Musketeer, whose tongue had become attached to his zipper.

"Morning, Jiggy McCue!" cried a hearty voice.

I turned. The man called Wallace was heading back across the road and Mr. Mann was waving at me from his shelter.

"Morning, Mr. Mann!"

"Thanks again for what you did the other day!"

"Anytime!" I said as the other two joined me.

Angie glared at me. "Terrific. Is that fair? I do some-one a really heroic good turn and you get the credit."

"That's life, Ange." I chuckled.

We turned a corner. The school was in sight. But so were Jolyon Atkins and his bonehead cronies. Spread out across the sidewalk waiting for us.

"Hi there, McCue," said Jolyon.

My knees did a sudden magic trick. They turned from knees into Jell-O. No particular flavor.

"Care to do another heroic good turn?" I said to Angie.

"Not me," she replied. "I haven't got enough testos-terone now to fluff up a cushion. Either grovel or take what's coming to you."

"It should be coming to you, not me."

"That's life, Jig," she chuckled.

I turned. I ran. So did Angie. So did the third Mus-keteer, the recycled one.

When at last we skidded to a heavy-breathing halt the school was once again in sight, but from a different direction and minus Atkins. The Jell-O between my ankles and personal places became knees again.

"So," Angie said. "All's well that ends well."

"For two of us anyway," I said, thinking of Pete, furry Pete, curled up in Stallone's basket back at The Dorks.

My mother had been so delighted to see him (or who she thought he was) that she'd taken the day off work to wait on him hand and foot. Pete had never been treated so well. Seemed to like the food that went with the job too.

"Fair average, two out of three," Angie said.

"Yeah. Could be worse."

I threw my arm out—my very own wonderful right arm—and pointed my very own wonderful finger at the road ahead.

"Onward, Musketeers. To school!"

"One for all . . ." said Angie.

"And all for lunch!" said I.

"Reowl," said the third Musketeer, and jumped up a tree after a bird.

JiGGY McCUE